CHAOS COMES

An After the EMP Novel

HARLEY TATE

CHAOS COMES

A POST-APOCALYPTIC SURVIVAL THRILLER

Two weeks into the apocalypse, would your switch be flipped?

Colt isn't a family man. As an air marshal, he doesn't have time for commitment. When his plane emergency lands outside of Eugene, Oregon, he knows it's the beginning of the end. When he sets off on his own, he's ready to face the future alone. Rescuing a kid isn't part of his plan.

When you have nothing left, can you find the will to survive?

Dani's only fifteen, but she's no stranger to hardship. When the pangs of hunger drive her to the brink, Dani makes the difficult choice to steal. She knows she might get caught. She never expects a stranger to save her.

The end of the world brings out the best and worst in all of us.

Colt and Dani will have to fight to survive in this post-apocalyptic world. Joining forces isn't part of the plan, but desperate times call for desperate measures. With danger around every corner, will they find the strength to trust each other? Or will the past ruin any chance of seeing the future?

The EMP is only the beginning.

Chaos Comes is book four in the *After the EMP* series, a post-apocalyptic thriller series following ordinary people trying to survive after a geomagnetic storm destroys the nation's power grid.

Subscribe to Harley's newsletter and receive an exclusive companion short story, *Darkness Falls*, absolutely free.
www.harleytate.com/subscribe

DAY SIXTEEN WITHOUT POWER

CHAPTER ONE

COLT

University of Oregon Campus
Eugene, Oregon
8:00 a.m.

The bed shifted beneath Colt's weight and he rolled to the side. Heather took up most of the bed, her hips teasing him beneath the threadbare sheet. At any other time in his life, Colt would have slid closer and enjoyed a little extracurricular start to his morning, but not today.

He sat up and scrubbed at the beard now coating his jaw.

According to the paper calendar on the wall, the nation's power grid failed just over two weeks ago. That's how long he'd been making due in Eugene, Oregon. A spit of a town centered around a college campus and not much more, it wasn't Colt's idea of a

2

good time. But then again, Heather had been a welcome distraction.

Being an air marshal, he'd always had a soft spot for flight attendants.

Heather murmured in her sleep and rolled onto her back and Colt admired the view. Red curls fanning out across the pillow, soft skin the color of milky tea, freckles unhidden by makeup. Part of him would miss waking up like this every day.

It had been a shock to watch the lights go out from cruising altitude above Oregon. Thanks to a quick-thinking pilot, the 747 emergency landed on a tiny little airstrip outside of Eugene. But even watching the blackout didn't prepare Colt for learning the truth on the ground: a massive EMP hit the United States.

The EMP didn't come from a terrorist attack or another country, but from the sun. He shook his head in wonder at it all. The same sun they relied on to stay alive had belched out a massive ball of gas so big, it caused an electromagnetic pulse large enough to fry the power grid across the country.

From what he'd been able to learn from the National Guard the past two weeks, things were bad. Real bad. Riots had shut down all the major cities coast to coast. Thousands of police, firefighters, and military personnel had abandoned their posts, desperate to get home to their families and protect them. Colt knew if he'd had a girlfriend or wife back home, he would have done anything to make it back.

But he wasn't a family man. No baggage. No weight. No compromises. That's how he lived his life ever since he became a SEAL, and that's how he would live it now that the world was knee-deep in a steaming pile of crap and sinking fast.

He thought about the pilot of the plane, Walter Sloane. Did he make it home to his family in Sacramento? Were they still alive today? Fear and panic had etched lines into the man's face as he said goodbye after landing the 747. Colt didn't blame him for leaving. Worrying about loved ones could tear anyone apart.

Lucky for Colt that wasn't a problem.

He stood up and slipped on his jeans, tugging up the worn and dirty denim before reaching for his shirt. As the black cotton slipped over his head, Heather murmured at him.

"Where are you going so early?"

No sense in sugarcoating it. "I'm packing up. Time for me to head out."

She sat up, clutching the sheet around her as she blinked herself awake. "Does the army have a job for you or something?"

Colt grabbed his shoes and perched on the edge of the bed, concentrating on his socks so he didn't have to look Heather in the eye. This wasn't about helping out the National Guard or the people of Eugene or even the SEALs. It was about leaving before he became attached and his choices were no longer one hundred percent his own.

He shoved one foot in a shoe and then the other. "I've been here long enough. It's time I hit the road."

The bed dipped as she scooted closer. "But I'm not ready to leave. We've got a place to sleep and so far there's been enough food and water for everyone here. The army has been good to us."

Colt tied his laces. "I'm leaving alone, Heather."

The responding silence seized Colt's insides, squeezing like an anaconda of regret. He sat for a moment, staring at his shoes, contemplating all the things he could say. He could throw out some platitudes and lies, a bit of puffery to ease the passage of the truth. But Colt wasn't that type of man.

Standing up, he faced Heather at last. She pressed her plump lips together and stared.

Colt waited.

"So that's it?" Heather broke eye contact and shook her head. "You shack up with me for two weeks and then you just walk out?"

"You knew it was temporary. I told you when you offered to share a room that I don't do relationships."

Her curls bounced as she scooted to the edge of the bed. "All men say that."

"I meant it."

"But where are you going to go? What are you going to do? The government has to be coming soon. This is a big town. There's a college here. They've got supplies and the National Guard and if we just wait it out, someone will come and help us."

"I wouldn't count on it." Colt grabbed his holster, fitting it inside his waistband before adding his service pistol. So many things had been nagging at him the past two weeks. He'd let them go because of Heather, but he couldn't any longer. "You should think about what you're going to do when the army's hospitality runs out."

Heather's eyes widened. "What are you talking about?"

"We've been lucky so far, but sooner or later, that will change." He dropped his voice. "There's something not right here, Heather. Where are all the college kids? The Townies? This campus should be teeming with people. Instead, it's just us—all the people from the plane who didn't leave—and the National Guard." He ran a hand through his hair. "It's going to get worse. A hell of a lot worse."

She shook her head. "You're talking crazy."

"No, I'm not."

Heather rolled her eyes and reached for her clothes on the floor and Colt turned around. He didn't want to fight with her, but he knew she would never see the world as he did. She would always believe someone out there would help her. So many people in the United States lived in a blissful ignorance about the rest of the world and the danger that lurked beyond their borders.

Colt had seen enough in his life to know what a farce such naive thinking could be. A crisis this big with no plans in place…

No one would be coming to help. Not ever. That the army was in Eugene at all surprised him.

He exhaled and reached for his duffel. Even if he wanted to bring Heather with him, she would never agree to go. She would cling to her hope until she didn't have the strength to hold on.

He waited until she'd finished getting dressed. "I'm

going to pack my things and head over to the cafeteria. You're welcome to come with me."

"You're making a mistake, Colt. Once the National Guard gets a handle on the riots in Sacramento, we'll be able to go home."

"Is that what you want? To go back to Sacramento?"

"Of course I do. I live there. My sister is there and her kids. I need to get home. As soon as they give us the all clear, that's where I'm headed."

"And how are you going to get there?"

She gawked at him. "In a vehicle, how else? I'm sure there will be buses taking people home soon. We just have to have faith."

Colt shook his head. He would never get through to her. He grabbed his bag and began shoving everything into it. First thing he needed to do when he got out of there would be to find a sporting goods store and secure a good backpack, more weapons, and gear.

It wouldn't be nearly enough, but it would be a start.

Heather stood at the edge of the bed, arms folded across her flight crew polo shirt, watching him. He hated to leave her mad and in denial, but he didn't see another way. She couldn't come with him.

Roughing it in the woods far away from civilization wasn't Heather's style. The woman still put on a full face of makeup every morning. They didn't have running water or flushable toilets, but she found a way to apply mascara.

Colt glanced up at her. "You should start gathering up some gear, Heather. A winter coat, some hiking boots. A flashlight. Maybe even a gun if you can find one."

"What would I need a gun for?"

"To protect yourself."

She snorted. "Don't be silly. No one will attack me."

He stood up and waited until she looked him in the eye. "You're a beautiful woman, Heather."

Her whole face lit up at the compliment.

"The longer this all goes on, the more of a target you'll become. Men will see you as an opportunity. A prize to be won."

Her smile slipped. "You're talking like this is the end of the world. Like we're all a few days away from *Mad Max*."

"We are."

She rolled her eyes. "After that show on the airplane, I knew you had a few screws loose, but Colt, seriously, this is too much."

He blinked. She didn't approve of how he handled the situation? "The man made terroristic threats on an airplane. I had to bring him in."

"He was harmless. You didn't need to draw a gun on him and lead him out in handcuffs. I know you guys like to make a big deal out of your jobs and all, but you could have tried talking to the guy."

Colt's jaw ticked. He *did* talk to him until the conversation incited panic among the other passengers. If he hadn't taken that guy off the airplane, all hell would have broken loose. They would never have taken off… and they would still be in Sacramento. Was that why she was so mad? Did she blame him for being stuck in Eugene?

He frowned. "I was doing my job."

"A little too well, if you ask me."

I didn't. Colt picked up his bag and slung it over his shoulder. A million thoughts swirled inside his head, none of them good. "Remember what I said, Heather. You need to prepare and stay vigilant."

"You'll see, Colt. In a few days, we'll be on the way back home and you'll be wishing you stayed right here on campus."

"For your sake, I hope you're right." Colt closed the distance between them in two strides. He knew now that whatever drew them together these past weeks, it wasn't real. They were just two people in the right place at the right time.

He unzipped his bag and pulled out a small folding knife. He wouldn't part with his service weapon, but Heather could have his backup. She needed a weapon. He grabbed her hand and set the knife in her waiting palm. "Take this. It's not a gun, but it's a good blade. It could save your life."

"Colt, I don't—"

"Just take it. For me."

She closed her fingers over the folded knife and nodded. "You sure I can't change your mind? That bed will be awful empty without you."

He nodded. "I need to go."

"Okay." She reached up and smoothed the front of his shirt, fingers lingering on the swell of his chest. "It was fun while it lasted."

"Yes, it was." Colt leaned in and kissed her lightly on the lips. "Be careful, Heather. And good luck."

"Good luck to you, too. When all of this blows over, come look me up in Sacramento, will you?" Heather stepped back and headed to the nightstand. She scribbled something on a scrap of paper and handed it to Colt.

Her phone number. Colt swallowed. No point in telling her it would probably never work again.

"Thanks, Heather." After one more kiss, Colt turned and headed toward the door. He'd spent the last two weeks in denial about the future, wrapped up in the arms of a woman who would never come to terms with this new reality. Vacation was over. Colt needed to get to work.

CHAPTER TWO

DANI

Sunnyvale Convalescent Hospital
Eugene, Oregon
9:00 a.m.

"Danielle, stop staring out that window and come over here."

Dani sighed and turned away from the glass to smile at her grandmother. No matter how many times she asked the seventy-nine-year-old to call her Dani, it didn't stick. "What is it, Gran?"

"You should eat. Come and have my applesauce."

"I'm not going to eat all of your food."

"Please, Danielle. I don't want it to go to waste."

Her grandmother pushed the little cup of applesauce across the tray table and Dani reluctantly picked it up. She peeled back the aluminum lid and stuck the plastic spork into the cup before shoving it into her mouth. The nursing home where her grandmother lived was low on everything.

Water. Food. Bathrooms.

Dani had been camping out there for the past week, hiding from the handful of employees who still made the rounds of the recovery wing and sharing her grandmother's dwindling meals. Dani didn't know if it was their proximity to the college campus, or the quick thinking of the staff, but this place had done all right for itself for the past two weeks.

But even her grandmother knew their time at Sunnyvale Convalescent Hospital was running short. As Dani finished the last of the applesauce, she turned her attention back to the window. From her grandmother's room on the third floor, she could see a few blocks across town to the stadium for the University of Oregon. National Guardsmen stood outside, rifles in their hands as they stood watch.

She had read enough books growing up that she knew those guys were the only reason the hospital hadn't been looted. Other parts of Eugene still smoldered. Thanks to her history class, Dani knew that at a hundred and fifty thousand people, Eugene was the second largest city in Oregon.

That meant Eugene had its fair share of thugs and the drugs to go along with them. She snorted as images of her mother came to mind. The world ended and her mother didn't even bother to come home.

She shouldn't care, but she couldn't help it. Dani turned around. "Do you think Mom will come home one of these days?"

Her grandmother clucked. "Don't you fret about your mother. That woman doesn't deserve your attention."

Dani chewed on her lip. How she wished Gran had never gotten sick. If only cancer hadn't reared its ugly head, they would still be living in that apartment uptown with working heat and food in the fridge and a good high school just down the street.

Life didn't ever seem to work out the way Dani wanted it.

Her grandmother interrupted her thoughts. "Your mother probably found somewhere else to stay."

Dani nodded. It wasn't the first time her mother had disappeared for days at a time. But with the power still out and no help other than the army, Dani wondered. *Where is she?*

The sound of footsteps down the hall caught her off guard and Dani rushed to the little closet. She slipped inside just as a familiar voice called out.

"Good afternoon, Mrs. Weber. I see you liked your lunch today. Good for you."

Gran cleared her throat. "Do you by any chance have any extra? I noticed the portions were a bit smaller today."

Dani strained to hear through the wood of the closet door.

"I'm afraid not. Our kitchen is still waiting on our delivery for this week. But don't you worry, I'm sure we'll be back up to full meals soon."

Sounds of the orderly flitting about the room, fluffing pillows and taking the tray table away, made

Dani's heart beat double-time in her chest. She didn't know what would happen to her if she got caught. Did foster care still exist? Juvenile detention? Worse?

All she knew was that a fifteen-year-old didn't get to make her own choices, even if she did a better job of it than her mother ever did.

At last, her grandmother gave the all clear and Dani stepped out of the closet. "That was close. I need to pay more attention."

"I still think we should tell them that you're here, my dear. I'm sure they would let you stay under the circumstances."

"No. We can't risk it. What if they call the police? I'll get taken to the station and when they can't find Mom, I'll get sent away. Maybe even detention." Dani tucked her hair behind her ear. "I'm still on probation, Gran. I can't risk it."

Her grandmother's wrinkled lips thinned to a line. "I still can't believe you stole those groceries. If you were hungry, you should have come to me. I would have helped you."

Dani stayed silent. She wasn't about to tell her grandmother about that day. "It doesn't matter. I just need to avoid the police, that's all."

"You sound like your mother."

Dani recoiled from the sting of her grandmother's words. "I'm nothing like her."

Gran exhaled and patted the edge of the bed. "I'm sorry, I didn't mean it. It's just... I have a bad feeling about all of this."

"So do I." Dani walked over to her grandmother's

bed and let Gran wrap her up in a hug. Gran's hair smelled like lavender and Dani wanted to curl on her lap and pretend she was five years old. "I don't think we can stay here much longer. The food is running out. I heard an orderly say the backup generators are running on fumes and they haven't been paid in over a week."

She pulled back and met her grandmother's patient gaze. "We're going to have to find somewhere else to go."

Gran reached for her hand. "I've been doing a lot of thinking, Dani…" She smiled, but it didn't reach her eyes. "I think you should go without me."

"No, Gran!" Dani tried to pull her hand away, but her grandmother gripped it tight.

"I'm an old woman in a hospital bed, Danielle. I'll only slow you down."

"That's no reason to give up. I can't just leave you here."

"Yes, you can. Besides, I need medicine. If I don't take my prescriptions, I'll die. It's as simple as that."

Dani yanked hard enough to free her hand as she stood up. "There have to be thousands of extra pills here. I can find them and convince the staff to give them to us." She paused. Her grandmother had to understand. "What if the staff leave and don't come back? Without someone bringing you food, you'll starve to death."

Her grandmother's eyes shimmered behind her glasses. "You're young. You have your whole life ahead of you. I'm an old woman, Danielle. Maybe this is my time to go."

"No." Dani refused to listen to another word. Her grandmother was the only good person in her life. She wasn't going to lose her. "If you won't leave, then I won't either. We'll both stay."

"You need more food. Water. I know how hungry you are. I can see it in your eyes."

Dani turned away. "Then I'll go out and look for some." She reached down for her backpack hidden beneath the bed. "I'll leave right now." She slung the bag over her shoulder and wiped at her face. Her grandmother didn't need to see her tears.

"Are you sure?"

"Yes." Dani turned around and forced a smile. "If you won't leave, then I won't either. Not until I have to. But that doesn't mean we can't have something better to eat. I'll be back before dark." She leaned forward and gave her grandmother a quick kiss on the forehead.

"Be careful, Danielle. We don't know how dangerous the world is now."

Gran might not, but Dani sure did. Spending three years living with a drug addict mother taught a girl a thing or two about surviving on the streets. Dani could keep them both alive; she didn't have another choice.

Without another word, Dani slipped out the door to her grandmother's room and made her way to the stairs. By her count, only three orderlies still worked this wing of the building. If she could time it right, she could get in and out without a single one seeing her.

After running down two flights of stairs, Dani eased the ground floor door open and listened. *Silence.* She pushed it open and slipped through, holding it until it closed. Maybe her grandmother was right and a simple conversation with the staff would mean she could come and go whenever she liked. But the longer the blackout went on, the meaner everyone would get.

It wasn't that different from a junkie coming down from a high without any money for another hit. Dani had seen it so many times, she knew all the signs. First the shakes. Then vomiting and diarrhea. Then the pleading and begging.

The sweetest words came out of her mom's mouth when she was fishing for a few extra dollars. She would screw up her face into what passed for a smile and reach out with shaky fingers.

"Your hair is so pretty today, Danielle… Did you do the laundry? Everything smells so nice… Any chance you have a few extra dollars from Grandma I can borrow?"

If the answer was no…

Punches always landed twice as hard after a compliment.

Dani shook off the memories. It didn't matter whether the staff of the nursing home would welcome her or call the cops, she didn't need them either way. She had Gran and that was enough.

Peering in the nearest room, Dani found what she was looking for: a ground-floor window. She eased inside the empty room and hurried to the glass. Facing the rear of the property and a row of bushes, no one would notice if it stayed unlocked and had a hole in the screen. She pushed it open, took the pocket knife from her backpack, and cut across the bottom of the screen.

In another minute, she was out the window and on the ground. She pushed the window back down and rushed to the edge of the building.

Food and water. Those were the necessities. If she could find a good stash, maybe they could stay in the nursing home until the power came back on or the place shut down. Either way, it would keep her grandmother alive.

That was what mattered.

CHAPTER THREE

COLT

COLT STRODE WITH PURPOSE THROUGH THE HALLS OF the University of Oregon. Thanks to spring break and the National Guard unit that set up shop on campus, Colt had managed to place all the passengers in temporary dorms.

After promising the pilot that he would take care of the passengers, it was the least he could do. When he'd secured the deal, Colt assumed they would all be there a weekend, tops. The power would come back on and the whole thing would be a giant misunderstanding. He'd seen crazy things like rolling blackouts and only one hour of electricity overseas, but in the United States? Never thought it would happen.

Sixteen days later, he embraced reality with both arms. This was still the early time. Millions of people around the country still lived in denial. Neighbors and friends banded together and shared resources. Churches opened their doors and took strangers in.

But soon, things would begin to change. He'd seen it in war-torn cities and refugee camps. Soon the strong would take advantage of the weak. Soon the people unprepared for the stark brutality of life without plenty would suffer.

Colt didn't want to be there when it happened. He had to get out.

His explanation to Heather had only been half of the truth. Leaving wasn't just about hitting the road as a single guy without anyone bogging him down. It was about survival.

Some of the things he'd seen and done in the navy…

He shook his head to clear it of the horrors of the past. His job brought baggage but knowledge, too. He could assess threats as they came and act accordingly. He could act and react without pausing to think.

A girlfriend would only complicate that. They always did.

He waved at the handful of people in the hall: a woman with her young daughter from row 14; a man with his teenage son from row 28, another crew member who decided to stay and not find a way home to Sacramento first thing.

All told, forty-seven other people stayed behind in Eugene after the plane made the emergency landing post-EMP. Forty-seven people sitting in their temporary rooms day after day waiting for someone to save them and make everything okay.

Nothing would ever be okay again.

Colt adjusted the duffel on his shoulder before pushing the door open to the outside. It felt good to breathe the cool Oregon air.

"Hey, Colt."

He turned and smiled at the man who called his name. "Hi Roger, how are you?"

Roger shrugged his oversized frame and squinted up at the sky. "It's not raining, so I guess it's a good day." Just promoted to sergeant a week before the blackout, Roger Gunther was a good kid who spent most of his time under the hood of a 1966 Mustang convertible. From the pictures he'd shown Colt, the car was a beauty. Too bad the kid wouldn't be using it any time soon.

"Out for some fresh air?"

The sergeant's face fell. "Have you heard anything about the restrictions we rolled out this morning?"

Colt paused. Restrictions meant trouble. "No."

Roger glanced at the space between the two buildings up ahead and Colt followed suit. A fellow National Guardsman paced back and forth in and out of Colt's field of view.

"Orders came down from Colonel Jarvis this morning. No one in, no one out. Authorized personnel only."

Colt frowned. "Were you trying to leave?"

Roger nodded. "I wanted to take a walk. Get out and see some of Eugene, meet some of the neighbors.

They told me only soldiers assigned to patrol could leave. Claimed we're on lockdown for security reasons."

"That doesn't make any sense." Colt squinted into the distance. "Isn't there already a mandatory curfew?"

Roger nodded. "Sundown to sunup. And the patrol units go out every night, driving up and down the streets, keeping everyone in check."

"Are there riots somewhere? A part of the city they don't have under control?"

Roger hesitated. "I'm not really supposed to say."

Colt nodded. The kid probably told him too much already. But the lockdown gave Colt pause. The military didn't enforce restrictions like that unless they expected to lose control of an area. Was Eugene about to fall like Sacramento?

He thought about the stories other guardsmen like Roger told him of Sacramento. One shaken-up private told him the whole city was on fire and they had been ordered to seal everyone inside. The good and the bad, it didn't matter. If a person was inside the riot area when the barricades went up, they didn't get to leave. No matter what.

If that was happening in a relatively calm place like Eugene, then it was happening all over. The only question in Colt's mind was whether the lockdown was intended to protect the people inside, or just keep them contained.

He glanced at Roger. "If you want to leave, you should do it now. Otherwise, just stay put and follow orders."

Roger nodded. "Thanks, Colt."

Colt said his goodbyes and watched Roger walk away. If what the sergeant said was true, Colt needed to get out before he had to fight his way out. No one was trapping Colt Potter behind a fence.

He strode toward the road, head up, eyes searching for potential conflicts. It had been a long time since he'd operated in the field, but his job as an air marshal forced Colt into a state of hyper-vigilance often enough that the skills came back in an instant.

Eugene wasn't a third-world village halfway across the country, but the threats would be the same before too long. When food and water ran out, ordinary people would turn desperate. Some probably already were. That a National Guard presence had mobilized so quickly in the area meant parts of the town had to be secure. A much better outcome than other cities.

Portland was chaos. Sacramento, San Francisco, Seattle. All worse than any town in the Middle East. Fires. Looting. Robbery. Murder. Crimes without punishment. People without any means to protect themselves.

Too many bad people in too small a space. Take away the law and order and chaos erupted in their place. From what Colt had seen inside the college campus, the National Guard had done a damn fine job in Eugene.

Rumors among the passengers claimed the army found a means to tap in to wind turbines on the coast and power the campus. That in a matter of days they would be turning the whole town back on. From what Colt had been able to discover, most of the power was being used by the army, but he hoped once they secured the campus, they would do their best to restore the power to the whole town.

Power made order possible. The mandatory curfew and supposed patrols full of armed men didn't hurt, either. Colt wondered how long the quasi-military state would last when the guardsmen didn't get paid and were told they couldn't go home. The more the area turned into an open-air prison, the more the local townspeople would rebel.

Some would start in secret, but some would be bold and out in the open. The first public skirmish would undermine the tenuous peace. A few poor decisions and it would disintegrate into something akin to a war zone. Battles for territory and control. Fights over limited resources and access to food and water.

Medicine and drugs would be worth more than life itself. What role would the diminishing military play in all of it? Colt hoped he didn't have to find out.

"Sir! Excuse me, sir!"

Colt slowed and turned his head. A National Guardsman approached, rifle held in a relaxed grip across his chest.

As the man approached, Colt glanced at his rank. "Is there a problem, Corporal?"

'Sir, my orders are to keep everyone inside the college campus. It's for your own safety."

Colt pulled out his wallet and flashed the air marshal ID. "I'm a United States air marshal. I've been here working to secure the safety of a flight that emergency-landed in the area, but now I need to leave and get back to work."

He took a step forward but the corporal's rifle swung out. "Sir, I'm sorry. My orders are to not let anyone in or out."

"Are you setting up barricades?"

"I…I can't confirm any information, sir. Please go back inside."

"No."

The corporal stared at him, unsure what to do.

Colt seized the opportunity and took a step forward. "What happens when someone refuses to obey? What are your orders then?"

"To detain and wait for assistance."

Colt shook his head and stepped to the side. "How old are you, twenty-two?"

"Twenty, sir."

"How many tours have you seen?"

"None, sir."

"Well before I became an air marshal, I was a SEAL. So how about you put that rifle down and let me walk out of here."

"I can't do th—"

Before the kid even finished his sentence, Colt closed the distance between them. He shoved the palm of his left hand out hard and fast, hitting the cover panel of the rifle as he swung up with his right. Colt's fist connected, sending the kid's head careening to the left.

Colt wrapped his hands around the rifle and slipped it out of the corporal's grasp. It was over in seconds.

The kid blinked, staring in shock at Colt before looking down at his empty hands. "How did you…"

"Skill. And a lot of practice." Colt glanced around. So far they were the only two on the road, but that could change any moment. "Now. I'd like to give this back to you, but I want to leave more."

The corporal swallowed. "If I promise not to shoot you, will you give my rifle back?"

"Will you let me leave?"

The kid's head bobbed up and down.

"All right. If you keep your word, I'll walk away and you'll never see me again. If you don't, you won't like what happens next."

He nodded again. "I'll keep my word. I promise."

"For your sake, I hope you do."

Colt checked the safety and gave the rifle back to the kid. "If I were you, I'd keep a better handle on my weapon. Just because you're holding it, doesn't mean someone isn't going to get the upper hand."

"Yes, sir."

Colt flashed the kid a smile and stepped into the street. He pretended not to notice that the tip of the rifle shook as he turned around. Ten feet away, he glanced back.

The poor guy still stood there, scared and dumbfounded, unable to do anything but gawk. He would either learn or die trying. Colt hoped it would be the former.

With a final wave, he took off, trotting down the street and out of sight of anyone on patrol.

CHAPTER FOUR

DANI

Downtown
Eugene, Oregon
10:00 a.m.

Whoa. Dani sucked in a breath. The first one in she didn't know how long. Her fingers tingled. The hair on her neck stood at attention. She watched the man in the black T-shirt disarm the military guy with a sleight of hand and a well-timed punch.

She'd never seen anything like it. He was dangerous. Awe-inspiring. But before she knew it, he'd handed the rifle right back to the guy and turned around.

He simply walked away.

Dani swallowed. How did he do it? If she ever tried something like that, she would end up shot or thrown in jail. Being fifteen and half his size might have something to do with that, but still.

She might be able to sneak past a ten-dollar-an-hour security guard with a candy bar in her back pocket, but disarm someone with a gun? No freakin' way.

Was he military, too? Some sort of secret agent man like Fox Mulder or Alex Krycek? When she lived with Gran, all she got to watch on TV were shows about sewing or painting or nature, except for reruns of *The X-Files*. Gran loved that show and Dani did, too.

The first few months after Gran moved to the nursing home, Dani used to sit in the kitchen window of her mom's apartment, daydreaming that she was Dana Scully, fighting bad guys with her partner all over the country.

After a while, the fantasies faded. It was hard to think about the future when you were focused on just surviving the next day. They didn't even have a TV. Her mother sold it to support her drug habit.

Dani shook her head to clear the fog of the past and climbed up the rear stairs of the corner store. Once she got old enough to walk down the street without catching the eye of the police or well-meaning busybodies convinced she was lost, Dani walked the three miles to the nursing home. Thanks to her weekly treks, she had learned the layout of the nearby streets.

Four blocks from the nursing home, the little store was one of those places that catered to broke college kids with bread and milk and a whole back wall of beer. It sat one block off the college campus in a building with painted brick walls and a bright-green awning out front.

Dani had been in it a few times to grab things for Gran with a handful of dollars the old woman scraped together somehow. But she'd never stolen from the place. Dani reserved that for the big places who wouldn't miss a granola bar or an energy drink.

Beggars couldn't be choosers, though. Her mom told her that over and over and over. When all they had was a bottle of ketchup and a can of tuna, that's what Dani ate. When they didn't have that…

She bit down on her tongue hard enough to draw blood. The metallic tang hit her taste buds and Dani inhaled.

Food and water and getting back to Gran was all that mattered. If only she could be a little bit like that guy from the street. She glanced down at her hands, fingernails grimy with dirt, half the cuticles red and torn.

Gran deserved someone better looking out for her. Someone like that stranger. But Dani would do the best she could. With a deep breath, she tugged her sweatshirt off and wrapped it around her hand.

Now or never.

She punched the window pane and it splintered. She hit it again and it broke, big jagged pieces falling all over the ground. It sounded like crystal gunshots, shattering the silence. Dani glanced up. Did anyone hear?

After a moment of waiting with nothing but the sound of her own breath as company, she stripped off the sweatshirt and reached inside the broken window and fumbled with the lock. It didn't budge.

Cursing, she stuck more of her arm inside, twisting her body to gain enough leverage to turn the lock. The broken glass cut her arm and she let out a cry. *Dude.* She couldn't even open a door without screwing it up. Dani began to pull her arm away, but the thought of Gran made her pause.

Gran needed her. She would just have to try harder.

Focusing on the pain in her arm and the lock, Dani closed her eyes to concentrate. She gripped the edge of the lock, tugging hard as she braced her body on the door for leverage.

It moved.

She exhaled in relief. A few more yanks on the lock and it released. She turned the knob and slipped inside.

Without power, the threat of an alarm or video feed was gone. That had always been her biggest fear before the lights went out. Were they watching her? Would someone in a back room see her slip a snack into her jeans? Would they come to get her?

That's how it happened the first time. The only time. Dani had been so hungry, she'd been sloppy and careless and half out of her mind.

The cop didn't care. The detention center didn't care. She didn't get something to eat until she passed out in the holding cell and slammed her head on the metal bench.

She reached up and ran her fingers over the scar. Thirteen stitches, a vending machine sandwich, and ten days in juvie. Dani put on five pounds. It had been the best ten days of ninth grade.

Running her hand along a hallway wall, Dani felt her way toward the front of the store. The hall ended with two doors. One felt cold and metal, the other wood. She opted for metal. Fire code meant metal doors for stairwells, wood for everything else. She knew that much.

Turning the handle, she held her breath. The door opened into darkness. Dani couldn't see a thing. She reached into her pocket and pulled out a lighter she'd pocketed before she left home.

After flicking it on, she held it out in front of her. *Yes!* Stairs.

She took them slow and quiet, easing down each one as the little flame wobbled in front of her.

Halfway down, the metal of the lighter grew too hot and she released it, plunging the stairwell into darkness. She felt her way down the rest of the way, one foot easing over the stair to the next one, again and again, until she hit the bottom floor.

Jamming her thumb down hard on the spark wheel, Dani lit the lighter again and gritted her teeth against the heat. She'd reached a tiny vestibule, no bigger than a coat closet with nothing but a metal door and walls.

She reached for the door with her free hand and turned the knob. It opened and she stuck the lighter out in front of her.

The store.

Dani lifted her thumb and the light extinguished. Thanks to the east-facing windows, she could see despite the paper covering the glass. The morning sun peeked through all the cracks and crevices, spilling into the store and lighting up row upon row of food.

Saliva pooled in Dani's mouth and she swallowed it down. Chips. Candy. Cookies. All of it would taste so good.

But Dani learned over time what to steal and what to leave behind. She wasn't there for a quick fix or a sugar rush. She needed things that would keep her full and keep her going.

Down the aisles she raced, head low and feet quiet, ever mindful of minimizing noise and movement. She found the energy bars and rushed to open one, shoving the chocolate-coated oats and nuts into her mouth as fast as she could.

It went down hard and she opened the closest drink —a bright green, no-name soda. Screw the water, she needed calories. Nutrition class had been such a waste in school. A perfect teacher with sensible shoes and a home-packed lunch lecturing her about empty calories.

Try no calories, Dani wanted to shout half the time. But she didn't. Instead, she nodded along, took the tests, kept her head down and hoped no one noticed her growling stomach when she stared at pictures of food. At least she ate school lunch. Monday through Friday, one meal a day.

Better than none.

She tore into another bar, shoveling it into her mouth much like the first. Only when she'd finished it off and the rest of the soda did she stop to breathe.

If the allure of food hadn't driven the fear from her mind and overpowered her senses, maybe she would have heard the lock turning or caught the flash of light.

But Dani didn't look up until too late.

CHAPTER FIVE

COLT

DOWNTOWN
Eugene, Oregon
10:30 a.m.

THE BROKEN GLASS CRUNCHED BENEATH COLT'S brown leather dress shoe and he reminded himself to find some boots. Good, sturdy ones with waterproofing and a steel toe. Boots he could kick a door down with and still hike for ten miles the same day.

He eased into the store avoiding the piles of tempered glass surrounding the empty window frame. At some point, he would have to sit down and think through his new situation. The last two weeks had been wasted. Tucked inside a dorm room with Heather, he could forget about society crumbling to pieces all around them.

But standing in the middle of a ransacked store, Colt

couldn't ignore reality. Even a small town like Eugene—where college kids usually dominated the streets and people still smiled at strangers—wasn't immune. How long before it turned into another Portland? How long before the fires burned long into the night and the good people of the town fought to survive?

Sixteen days without power and some must be desperate. Were they starving? So thirsty they resorted to stealing? Cole reached for the butt of his pistol and touched it for reassurance.

He didn't have the same qualms about right and wrong in emergency situations. At least not when it came to resources. He wouldn't take more than he needed or waste those items he didn't use, but Colt would steal. If stealing kept him alive, then he had a chance to pay it forward. Someone out there would need help and he would give it.

So many TV shows showed people turning vicious and cold the minute the power went out or the apocalypse happened. Colt had been in situations just as bad or worse. It didn't turn him into the bad guy. If anything, it made him more aware of the need to be human and have compassion.

But only toward those he could trust or neutralize. Someone threatened him? Forget it.

He looked around him at all the senseless destruction. Someone busted the front window and stormed in, probably heading straight for the beer cases that now stood empty. *Idiots.*

Soon money would be worthless and trading would be essential. He needed things of value that people would pay dearly to acquire. In the military, guys were always trading: gear, supplies, food. The more time he spent in the field, out in some dust bowl of a country, talking to locals and gathering intel, the more trading became a critical part of life.

Barter always sat better with him than outright theft. Unfortunately, he was miles from home with nothing of value. He'd have to start with theft and work his way up.

He kicked at a toppled-over circular stand that once held a hundred bags of chips. Bypassing the remaining candy, chips, and pretzels, he went straight for the wall behind the register. He stopped in front of the Plexiglas case and smiled. So many cigarettes.

They were practically priceless. From the scratches on the plastic, it appeared someone already tried to get in without success. The two-inch padlock and tamper-resistant case kept ordinary thieves out, but not Colt.

Half of his buddies from the navy knew crazy ways to open locks using everything from strips of soda cans to a pair of wrenches and a lot of upper body strength. Colt preferred the path of least resistance.

He turned to the counter and felt around the dark space beneath it, fingers running over curled magazines and a tin of dip before settling on the item he needed. *Keys*.

Colt plucked them from the shelf before selecting the most likely candidate. *Bingo*. The lock popped open, he pushed the Plexiglas back, and Colt had access to hundreds of boxes of cigarettes without making a single noise or spending an afternoon frustrated or sweaty. *Always try the easy way first.*

After grabbing a plastic shopping bag, he fluffed it until the smiley face on the side showed off a full grin and stuffed the cartons inside, ten in all. He would have loved to take more, but without a means of easy transport, this would have to do.

The Plexiglas slid back into place with ease and Colt locked it up before pocketing the keys. No sense in giving anyone else unfettered access. Now that he had something to trade, he could turn to more obvious needs like food and water. He grabbed as many bottles of water as he could squeeze into his already-full carry-on duffel from the plane, a handful of power bars, mixed nuts, and jerky. With all of it, he could make do for a few days. A week, if he had to.

He skirted a knocked-over display case and shook his head. The things people stole never made sense. Warm beer, chips, and candy bars. Sunglasses and key chains and every kind of doodad on the market. All temporary highs that didn't mean anything in the long run. Those same people had empty cupboards and hungry bellies two days later.

Colt paused and looked around. The obvious had been taken, but what about the rest? Were there things he could use? He walked to the rear of the store toward the miscellaneous aisle that held everything from antifreeze to baby wipes and everything in between.

After shaking open another grocery bag, Colt filled it. First a map of the area, then a little flashlight, batteries, a pack of bungee cords and zip ties. He wished he could take the motor oil, but there wasn't any room.

As the shelves transitioned to cleaning supplies, Colt grabbed hand sanitizer and wipes and toilet paper. Vaseline and cotton balls and dental floss. There were so many things that could come in handy, but Colt had enough. He never took the last of anything and he only took enough to see him through this initial burst of hardship.

Whatever happened in the coming weeks and months, he would have to find a place to hunker down and set up camp. Only then would he forage for more supplies or work on necessary trades. For now, he needed his wits and easy transport. He turned and looked out the broken window.

The college bookstore sat behind the National Guard's new perimeter, but it would have everything he needed. A solid backpack. A hat and a raincoat to survive the sudden rain that seemed to come out of nowhere up here.

It meant risking a trip back inside, but what choice did he have? If he didn't find a local off-campus place that had what he needed, the bookstore would be his next stop. Colt waded through the wreckage toward the front of the store. He caught a glimpse of his reflection in the unbroken section of glass and paused.

Loaded down with plastic shopping bags and an overfull duffel, he looked every bit the thief. He wasn't any better than the hoodlums who smashed the place. He didn't break down the front window, but he still availed himself of the opportunity.

But what choice did he have? Over a hundred miles from home with nothing but the clothes on his back and a carry-on, Colt wasn't prepared for the end of the world. He could choose to leave everything where it sat and attempt to survive without food or water or any supplies, but that would be a death sentence.

He could go back to the college and sit around with idle hands, waiting for the other shoe to drop. What if the army confiscated his weapon? What if they put him to work in some sort of labor camp? What if they just walked away when the food ran out and the college wasn't useful anymore?

No. Colt was a survivor. He would take what he needed and let go of the guilt. Pass it forward when he could.

Stepping out of the store, he held his head high. As he turned the corner of the building, he came face-to-face with his first glimpse of the future.

CHAPTER SIX

COLT

Downtown
    Eugene, Oregon
    11:00 a.m.

"Let me go!" The high-pitched voice echoed off the brick wall beside Colt's head and he ducked into the shadow of the building.

"No f'ing way."

"I didn't do anything!"

"Bullshit. You were in that store stuffing your face full of food that doesn't belong to you."

"I was gonna pay for it!"

Colt eased back toward the broken window and deposited his things in the darkness beyond the glass. Whoever was out there didn't need to see his haul of cigarettes and beef jerky. At least not yet. He slipped his

Sig out of his holster and checked to confirm it was ready to fire.

A little voice in his head told him to grab his crap and get out of there, but Colt couldn't. The person screaming to be let go sounded way too young to be treated like a criminal.

He eased down the street, eyes sharp for any movement. Urban reconnaissance was the worst. Too many windows and doors. Countless places to hide. It made accurate threat assessments almost impossible.

Two feet from the corner, he paused. The voices picked back up.

"Don't touch me!"

Shit. Colt eased forward and pulled his sunglasses off the top of his head. He held them out at an angle, just past the brick corner of the building and tilted them until he could see. Mirrored lenses had so many advantages.

From his distorted view, it appeared a single soldier held a scrap of girl by the backpack, and the little thing was giving him a serious run for his money. The soldier was so caught up keeping the girl at arm's length, he never looked up. Not once.

Colt pulled his glasses back and slipped them on before easing close enough to peer around the corner.

"Please, mister, just let me go!"

"Not a chance, sweetheart. You're going straight to lockup. By the look of you, I bet you've gone there a million times."

What a jerk. The soldier couldn't have been much older than the one he disarmed half a mile down the road, but this guy had a hard-on for some action. With his rifle slung over his shoulder, he couldn't even defend himself properly. All he cared about was punishing some kid for finding a way to stay alive.

Colt frowned. He couldn't stand guys like this.

From the looks of the girl, she'd been hungry a while. Sunken cheeks. Stringy hair. The wild, feral look kids get when they've gone too long without.

He'd seen it too many times across the world: kids with old faces and bottomless eyes.

The girl twisted in the soldier's grasp, her arms locked down across her chest to keep the straps of her backpack on her shoulders. The army jerk kept trying to unzip her pack, but with one hand holding the top handle, he couldn't secure enough leverage to get it open.

"Hold still, damn it!"

"No! Let me go!"

The soldier cursed again and pulled his arm back. Colt tensed as the guy's palm landed smack on the girl's head.

"I said, hold still. Don't make me ask again."

Colt hesitated. Although he could make the shot, the soldier didn't deserve a bullet. Maybe if Colt revealed himself, he could talk the guy down, but it might end up in a fight. Would the kid even be thankful? Did she want to be rescued?

He wasn't much for saving helpless things.

The girl stilled enough for the soldier to open her backpack and he whistled in appreciation. "Well, look what we have here." He pulled out a box of Slim Jims. "These sure will come in handy back at the base."

"Those are mine." She twisted in his grip, but he leaned in close and she ducked her face away.

"That's right. I'm the one in charge. Consider everything in this backpack payment for the grief you've put me through."

Colt rolled his eyes. He should walk away. The girl didn't mean anything to him and helping her would only expose him to risk and potential injury. She wasn't a fighter. Not, really. One good hit and she'd already cowered into submission.

Bringing his pistol back, he began to move away from the corner when an anguished cry tore from the girl.

"Stop! That's for Gran. It's not yours!" She scrabbled at the man's hands where he held a six-pack of some drink in his hands. "She needs it!"

"You got an old lady to take care of? Shit, little girl, she's gonna be dead in a week with no one but you lookin' out for her. She won't mind if I help myself to her stash."

In an instant, the girl's demeanor changed. Gone was the shrinking violet and in her place, a fighter. She twisted in the soldier's grip and brought her knee to her chest.

Colt inhaled and found his focus. Everything slowed.

The girl's foot came down hard on the soldier's knee and Colt watched the joint buckle and warp. A shout ripped from the man's lungs as his leg gave way, but he didn't release his grip on the backpack.

If only she let the bag go, she could get away. She would be free.

But the stubborn kid wouldn't give it up. She slipped her arms out and spun around before yanking on it with all her might. The soldier groaned and landed hard on the ground, but he didn't let go. He grabbed for his rifle with one hand while he held onto the backpack with the other.

"You're about to wish you never set foot in that store, little girl."

That's it.

Colt couldn't let a kid who was trying to keep herself and someone else alive get shot. Not when he could do something about it. He stepped clear of the building with his gun pointed straight at the soldier.

"Drop your weapon!"

The girl spun, dirty dishwasher hair flying wide in an arc as her mouth fell open. Her hands still clutched the backpack, but her eyes were trained on his gun.

"I said, drop your weapon."

"Or, what? You gonna shoot a man in uniform?" The soldier tried to puff himself up with one knee on the ground and the other contorted in pain. "You really want that hell on your shoulders?"

Colt didn't blink. "Are you really going to shoot an unarmed little kid? How are you going to explain that to Colonel Jarvis?"

The soldier faltered, the barrel of his M-4 dipping as he worked his jaw back and forth. "Who are you?"

Colt stepped closer. "You don't want to know who I am. Drop your weapon."

The girl stood, petrified and still, staring at Colt like the Red Sea parted at his feet.

One shot would end this. One bullet to the asshole's head and the girl could run and Colt could be on his way. But he didn't want to shoot anyone.

Colt knew the rotten streak ran deep inside the man. One look at the sneer on his face and the calculating look in his eyes as he positioned himself behind the kid and Colt had him pegged. He wasn't one of the good guys. He was one of those SOBs who joined the military to shoot people, not to keep the country safe or do his duty. Like a bad cop on a power trip, the guy would always be trouble. Using a kid as a shield was pathetic.

Colt made a show of aiming the Sig. "I won't ask again."

After a tense standoff for what seemed like minutes, the soldier caved. He shrugged the strap of the M-4 off his shoulder and shoved the rifle across the pavement. "I'm gonna catch hell if you take that."

Colt reached down and picked it up. "Should have thought about that before you picked on someone half your size." He slipped the rifle over his neck and arm and slung it behind him. "Now let her go."

"She's a thief. She should be punished."

"By whom? You?"

"The authorities."

Colt snorted. "And who would that be, exactly? I don't see any cops around. Or lawyers or judges or anyone who gives a damn. Your unit doesn't have time to play jail warden."

"What do you know about my unit?"

"I know you're locking down the college campus. Is that to keep the bad people out or the good people in?"

The soldier broke eye contact. "I don't know what you're talking about."

Part of Colt wanted to push the issue. The way the guy ducked his head meant he knew something, but the girl needed saving. She stood like a statute in a garden, still and unmoving, while the two of them traded insults. She should be somewhere safe. Didn't she have anyone to take care of her?

He pushed the thoughts aside. Dealing with the girl would come later. "Let her go and hobble out of here and I won't tell Colonel Jarvis about this little incident."

The soldier chewed on his lip and glanced around him. They were still alone. "How do I know this isn't all some sort of act? You could be a nobody."

"Would a nobody be able to walk out of the college campus free and clear? Would a nobody be prepared to drop you where you kneel and not think twice?"

After a moment, the guy's shoulders sagged and Colt knew he'd won.

"Fine. I'll let her go." His fist opened and the girl moved like the Flash to stand a few feet away.

With a grunt of pain, the soldier pushed himself up to stand, hopping when his knee threatened to give way. "I should have hauled your scrawny butt in when I had the chance."

The kid stuck her tongue out at the soldier and Colt suppressed a chuckle. "Get on with it. You so much as open your mouth and you'll hit the pavement before a single word comes out. Understood?"

The soldier scowled at Colt, but nodded. Colt and the kid stood in the street, watching the injured soldier hop onto the sidewalk.

After he disappeared out of sight, Colt turned to the girl. "Mind telling me what the hell that was all about?"

CHAPTER SEVEN

DANI

Downtown
Eugene, Oregon
12:30 p.m.

Dani stared at the man in the black T-shirt through strands of her hair. What was he? Some kind of commando? One of those Special Forces guys no one ever talked about but everyone knew existed?

She ran her tongue over her teeth like she had a piece of food stuck in them, buying herself some time. During the past three years living with her mom, she'd learned not to trust anyone. He might have saved her, but that didn't mean he didn't bring something worse to the table.

Would he kidnap her? Hold her hostage? She stared at the pistol in his hand like it might leap up and bite her.

"I'm going to ask you again, what was all that about?"

Dani flicked her gaze up to his face. She couldn't see anything behind his mirrored sunglasses, just a bronze version of herself, distorted and smudged. His shoulders were relaxed, his body at ease with two guns and who knew what else lurking in his pockets. He knew how to handle himself.

She was no match for a guy like him. She couldn't run or hide or even think about getting away. Not unless she caused a commotion.

At last, she answered. "I was hungry. He caught me eating."

"Where?"

She hedged. "A store."

"Do you live around here?"

"No."

"Then what are you doing here? Do you need some help?"

"No." She shifted her weight, eyes never leaving the gun he still pointed.

The man exhaled in a burst and lowered the weapon. "How about you come with me out of the street? We can talk. I might be able to help you."

"No."

"Is that all you know how to say?"

Dani let a small smile tease the edges of her lips. "No."

The man laughed at that and pushed his sunglasses up his head. "I'm Colt." He stuck out his hand, the thick slab of flesh hanging in the midday sun.

She stared at his palm, wide and strong. If he didn't kill her, he could keep her safe. But she was better off alone. "Dani." She tucked her hair behind her ear to get it out of her face, but she didn't shake his hand.

Colt dropped it with a nod. "Come with me. There's a store around the corner that still has some food in it. You can finish filling up that backpack."

"I don't trust you."

"Good." He held his pistol low and loose at his side. "You shouldn't trust anyone now."

Dani frowned. He didn't seem like the rapist type. Or the kind to turn around and sell her to the highest bidder. She'd heard all about the dangers of human trafficking thanks to a school assembly last year. A woman had come and stood in the cafeteria, talking about all the predators kids could meet online and how so many never came home.

For a minute Dani had entertained the idea. How could anything be worse than her mom? But then the woman shared her own story and Dani went home thankful that night. At least her mom ignored her some of the time. Being hungry and alone beat what that woman faced at sixteen.

Colt glanced around. "We really should get out of the street before that guy comes back with his friends."

"So that part about knowing his boss?"

"Was a bit of an exaggeration. If you're coming, let's go. Otherwise, I'll see you around, kid." Colt turned to go, never once looking back.

Dani stood in the street, watching until he disappeared around the corner. Something about losing sight of the man tore up her insides and she took off, loping toward the corner of the building with her backpack still in her hands.

As she rounded the corner, she caught sight of him ducking through a busted window. She followed.

The place had been trashed. What used to be a little convenience store now looked like the after-effects of a riot or a bomb. The back wall of coolers stood open and empty, every case of beer stolen.

The revolving stands of sunglasses were rifled through and tipped over, bits of broken plastic sprawling out across the floor. Even the gum and candy were looted, all that remained were a few tins of Altoids and a 100 Grand bar.

Colt watched her as she picked through the store, waiting. At last, she turned to him. "So why did you rescue me?"

He raised an eyebrow. "Maybe I was hoping for a little appreciation."

Her cheeks warmed and Dani focused on the ground. He'd saved her from that creep and she hadn't even told him thank you. *I'm such a jerk.*

"Thank you for helping me. And for not being a serial killer or a pedophile." She glanced up and caught his eye. "You aren't, are you?"

Colt shook his head. "Neither. Just a guy who can't stand to see a bully take advantage of someone half his size, that's all."

Dani nodded. "Then, thank you. But you don't have to do anything else. I can handle myself." She set her backpack on the ground and began to repack it, shoving the six-pack of Ensure into the bottom before putting the trail mix and jerky back inside. The whole time she worked, Colt's eyes stayed on her, boring a hole in the sweatshirt she wore despite the spring heat.

The entire time she packed, she tried to ignore him, focusing on the backpack and her supplies instead of the commando-turned-security guard taking up space inside the store.

After a few more minutes, she couldn't take it anymore and turned to face him. He leaned back against the wall and crossed his arms over his chest. She frowned at him. "What?"

He shrugged. "Nothing."

She groaned and shook her head. "No way. You're thinking something. Nobody stands around like a bodyguard waiting around for no reason if they don't have an opinion."

Colt pushed off the wall. "Fine. Maybe I do have an opinion, but it's not one you'd want to hear."

"What's that supposed to mean?"

"Just what I said. It's not my place to tell you what to pack or what supplies you might need. You don't know me."

"You're right, I don't. Like I said, you could be a murderer or a drug dealer or... a cop."

Colt let out a chuckle. "You put the cops in the same categories as criminals?"

Dani focused on the half-empty rack of paper products in front of her. "Most of the time they're worthless. The other times they only make it worse."

"Then you haven't met the right ones."

Great. "Is that what you are? A cop?"

He shook his head. "Nope. But I've known enough of them to know they aren't all bad. Some of them are downright saints."

"Not around here, they aren't."

"So you do live around here."

Darn it.

"You don't have anything to fear from me, Dani. I'm not a threat."

"I don't know that. I don't know anything about you."

"True." Colt pushed off the wall and reached down to the floor. Up came a duffel bag that he slung over his body next to the rifle and a pair of shopping bags stuffed to the brim. "But I'm the best bet you have of making it home in one piece."

"I don't need your charity."

"No charity. Just company." He adjusted the duffel and glanced outside. "And a bit of protection."

Dani scowled. She couldn't take him to the nursing home and to Gran. She didn't know anything about the man. What if he turned her in when they got there? What if he was feeding her a bunch of bull just to take advantage of her when the moment was right?

"You walk me home and that's it, right? You'll let me go?"

"I'm not keeping you prisoner. You can go without me."

She zipped up her backpack and slung it over her shoulder. "I can?"

He nodded. "I just don't think you'll get very far."

He had a point. What if that military guy came back? What if she ran into someone worse? There was only one place she could take him. A place she hadn't been since the power quit out of fear of what she would find. But with a guy like Colt there, maybe it wouldn't be so bad.

"All right. Let's go." She led him out of the store and down the small side street. "I'll warn you, it's a long walk. Most people take the bus, but…"

"Transportation's a bit of an issue these days."

She nodded.

"It's fine. I need the exercise."

After a few blocks, they fell into step, Colt a few paces behind, head always up and eyes alert. Every once in a while, Dani would steal a glance behind her to make sure he was still there. Every time he gave her a nod and resumed his surveillance. He seemed like a guy straight out of the movies.

One of those FBI types who helped people out of bad situations when everything seemed hopeless. But no one was like that in real life. Everyone had baggage. Secrets.

Dani learned a long time ago that nothing was as simple as it seemed at first. They walked in companionable silence for almost an hour until Dani slowed. She pointed up at the dingy gray building with a call box out front.

"This is your place?"

She nodded. "My mom's." Dani glanced up at the building with a mixture of hope and dread. "You've seen me home. You can go now."

Colt lifted up his glasses and peered at the windows above them. "Naw, I think I'll walk you inside, make sure the place is safe, if that's okay."

Dani shrugged. He might as well know where she came from. Pride didn't keep her safe. But she needed to warn him about what he might find. She motioned to the holster on his hip. "You might want to be prepared. My mom can sometimes…"

She trailed off, unsure what to say.

Colt drew the pistol and nodded. "Thanks for the heads up. Lead the way."

CHAPTER EIGHT

COLT

489 BELLWETHER STREET
Eugene, Oregon
2:00 p.m.

IF THE TATTERED NAME TAPES ON THE CALL BOX WERE
any indication of the type of residents at 489 Bellwether
Street, Dani had been right to warn him. The whole
area looked one step up from the ghetto. No way the
army had made it this far in their patrols. From where
he stood, Colt counted five busted-out windows, new car
up on blocks, and two buildings burned from the
inside out.

Riots had already gripped this part of Eugene. He
wondered how many people were still left.

As Dani fumbled with a key for the scratched and
scuffed front door, Colt squinted to look through the
glass. Dilapidated cardboard boxes leaned against one

wall like a row of laborers who toiled all day in the sun, the backs bent and soaked in sweat. An empty counter that once held a doorman sagged beside a shabby set of stairs. Run-down was the charitable way to describe the place Dani called home.

She pushed the door open and the smell forced Colt to hold his breath.

Garbage. Lots of it.

He slipped in behind Dani and the putrid odor almost knocked him smack on his butt. "What *is* that?"

She winced at his words. "I guess no one's taking out their trash." She pointed at a hallway toward the rear of the lobby where bags spilled over each other in a stinking heap. "The dumpster's out that way, but it looks like there's a backup."

"Why didn't someone set the bags outside? Then the place wouldn't smell like this." *Ugh*. He brought his arm up to his nose, but it did nothing to ward off the smell.

Dani shrugged, but he caught the frown on her face. He shouldn't ride the girl so hard. He shoved down a wave of nausea and tried to lighten the mood. "The people who live here… They're not big on housekeeping, I guess?"

"Something like that." Dani walked through the lobby and started up the ragged stairs. Years of foot traffic had worn holes in a faded red carpet, exposing fifty-year-old linoleum beneath. The middle of each stair sank with use and Dani kept to the edges, trying to step where fewer feet had gone before. This wasn't her first time.

Something inside Colt began to ache. A low throb that echoed with every step. She wasn't the first kid he'd seen living in a situation like this, but she was the first one he felt an obligation to help.

Maybe because all the others had been while on active duty or because he'd been halfway around the world with more than a language barrier between him and all the little faces peering out of doorways and windows without glass.

The paint in the hall, once white, now streaked yellow from fingers and smoke. The railings were mostly black from a million greasy palms.

It was the kind of place reserved for drug addicts and their dealers, not a fifteen-year-old with clear eyes and a backpack full of food for someone else. Colt eased up the stairs a few behind Dani, letting her slight frame lead the way. She paused before stepping onto the third-floor landing.

Holding herself still with one arm wrapped around her middle, she clutched the key to the apartment like it could teleport her out of there. Whatever waited inside, she didn't want to face it alone.

Colt stopped beside her. "Maybe I should go first."

With a shake of her head, she refused. "No. I should do it. If Mom is home and she sees you, she'll freak." After a another moment, Dani stepped forward, her feet steady even though her hand never left her middle. So young and so brave.

She stopped outside apartment 304 and knocked loud enough to be heard down the hall. "Mom? It's Dani. I'm coming in." She unlocked the door and pushed it open. The door swung on squeaky hinges to reveal an apartment even worse than the hall. A bag of trash sat by the front door, half open and stinking, pizza boxes and beer cans spilling onto the dirty floor.

"Mom?" Dani took a step forward, but Colt shot out his arm. He couldn't let her go in there unprotected. Not based on his glimpse of the place.

"Let me go first. Just to clear it."

She hung back with a frown and Colt entered the apartment. It started with a hall, long and dark without any overhead lights. "Do you have a flashlight?"

"I've got a lighter."

Colt shook his head. "That won't work. All it will do is blind you." He crept forward, gun held comfortably down at his side. "Hello?" He called out. "Is anyone home?"

Even an addict riding a high would have heard his booming question. He eased down the hall to the living room. It opened in front of him and the sight fell like a brick into his stomach. Dani rushed past him to open the sagging brown curtains, stained from smoke and grime.

Sunlight fell on the coffee table and Colt forced his lips not to curl in disgust. Tented foil sat on the table, burn marks snaking down the middle, a lighter tossed beside it. Empty corner-cut bags littered the pocked wood tabletop.

He motioned to the mess. "This all your mom's?"

Dani nodded, eyes never leaving the obvious signs of drug use. "I never touch the stuff."

"Good." Colt brushed past the couch and entered

the tiny kitchen. He sucked in a breath before opening the fridge, but he didn't need to. The only thing inside was an empty jar of pickles and a single can of beer. He shut it and glanced around.

No food in the cabinets. Nothing to drink on the counter. "Did you eat everything before you left?" He hated to ask the question, but Colt had to know. How bad did this kid have it?

Dani picked at the sleeve of her sweatshirt. "Mom wasn't big on groceries."

Damn. "Where are the bedrooms?"

"There's only one." She stuck out her thumb toward the right. "It's down the other hall."

Colt followed where Dani pointed, clearing a tiny bathroom covered in grit and mold before heading into the bedroom. *God.* A mattress sat on the floor, sheets gray with dirt and soil haphazardly thrown on top. A dresser sat in the corner, piled high with empty beer cans and liquor bottles.

A hollowed-out light bulb with burn marks sat on the floor beside the bed. Colt bent to pick it up. *Meth.* It had to be. He set it down and strode back into the living room. Dani hadn't moved.

"Is that everything?"

She nodded.

"Where do you sleep?"

She pointed to the threadbare couch, worn to the stuffing on both arms. "My mom can't afford a two-bedroom."

Colt couldn't bear the thought of leaving this kid

here, alone. What if her mother came back? He turned and glanced again at the empty kitchen. What if she didn't?

He swallowed. A kid? He wasn't cut out to raise a kid. Not before the power grid failed and certainly not after. He couldn't be a father to her, but he couldn't leave her there either.

She looked so small standing in the light of the afternoon sun, her dirty hair highlighting gold in places. If she cleaned herself up and ate a million sandwiches, she'd be cute. A good kid that didn't deserve to live like this.

Embarrassment and shame rolled off her in waves as she focused on the floor. Her fingers never stopped rubbing the hem of her sweatshirt, the little motion like a knife into Colt's conscience.

If he left her there on her own, what kind of a man would he be? Not worthy to be called a SEAL. Not worthy to be called a man at all.

He scrubbed a hand down his face and exhaled. "How about you come with me?"

Dani jerked her head up, eyes wide and shimmering with unshed tears. "I can't do that."

"Why not?"

She swallowed. "I have reasons."

Colt rubbed at his temple. He had to get through to her. She needed to understand her options. He tried not to let his disdain infect his words. "Your mom, is she good to you?"

Dani looked away.

"Damn it, Dani. You can't stay here. There's no food, no water. It's not safe."

"I can—"

Colt held up his hand to cut her off. "Just hear me out, okay? I'm not a family man. I don't do kids or relationships or dogs or any of that stuff. It's always just been me and me alone. I don't want to be your surrogate dad."

Her eyes narrowed. "Then what do you want?"

"I can protect you. As long as you're with me, no one will hurt you. I can promise you that."

Dani's brows furrowed, shielding her brown eyes from his patient stare. She focused on him for so long, Colt wondered if she was working up the courage to say no.

At last, her chin shot up. "I'm not alone."

Colt remembered her plea to the soldier in the street. "Your grandmother?"

She nodded.

"Where is she?"

"Sunnyvale Convalescent Hospital. It's by the college."

"Then we'll go get her."

"You mean just walk in and wheel her out?"

Colt nodded.

Dani shook her head. "It's not gonna be that easy."

CHAPTER NINE

COLT

Downtown
   Eugene, Oregon
   3:30 p.m.

"YOU LIVED WITH HER UNTIL YOU WERE TWELVE?"

Dani nodded as she walked beside Colt, her posture more relaxed every block they moved closer to the nursing home. "We lived in a little apartment across town. It was small, but there were two playgrounds and a basketball court, and I could walk to the library."

"Sounds great." Colt couldn't imagine growing up in a place like that only to end up living in the squalid apartment they had left behind.

Dani didn't say anything for a while and Colt wondered if he'd brought up painful memories. He still didn't understand how her mother fit in to all of this. "So, your mom…"

"She's got some problems. When she went to prison the first time, that's when Gran took me in. I was four."

Colt couldn't imagine a toddler in that hellhole Dani's mother called a home. "Was your mom living in that place back then?"

Dani shook her head. "No. She had a job. A real good one working the cash register at a service shop." Dani's voice dropped a bit and Colt leaned closer to listen. "But she never had good luck with men. One of her boyfriends was a real jerk. Gran said he beat her up real bad. Put her in the hospital."

Her voice quivered and Colt guessed he shouldn't push her anymore. Whatever her story, he'd learn it eventually.

Colt went back to canvassing the neighborhood. The closer they got to the college, the quieter everything became. No kids out playing. No people chatting on their front porch. It didn't make any sense. It went from burned-out crack shack to ghost town in less than a mile.

About five blocks back, they'd come across a couple of men gathered in the shadow of a tree, heads together, speaking low. But the minute they saw Colt and Dani, the pair rushed off, ducking into a side entrance basement and out of sight. They acted afraid.

Colt brushed it off. He couldn't do anything about a couple of strangers now. Dani walked beside him, kicking at the pavement and keeping her eyes on the road. They were a few blocks from the college when Colt saw the familiar camouflage at the end of the street.

He grabbed Dani's arm. She started to protest, but Colt put his finger up to his lips. "There's an army guy at the next block. We should hide."

Dani's pale cheeks flushed and she nodded, all of a sudden looking so much younger than her fifteen years. "Where should we go?"

Colt glanced around. They were in the middle of a mixed-use area, half residential, half business. "Let's use the alley behind the shops. Maybe we can skirt around him."

He led Dani toward the small road barely big enough for a compact sedan. He was the third one they had avoided so far. Always a single, armed guardsman, canvassing the area on foot. Were they there to only keep order or was something else going on? Colt didn't know and he didn't want to find out.

As soon as he figured out how to ensure Dani's safety, he would hit the road. She was a good kid, but he'd told her the truth: he didn't do family.

They crouched behind a rank dumpster and Colt put on a smile. "Okay, Dani. You stay hidden right here and I'll check it out."

She opened her mouth, but Colt shook his head. "Don't even think about coming with me. He could be dangerous. It could be the guy who caught you before or someone else we don't want to run into."

"But if it isn't, then we don't need to hide."

"You don't know that. There aren't many people out on the streets. I've been inside the college since I got here; I don't know what's going on out here. For all I know, the army could have standing orders to detain anyone they meet. We can't risk it."

She palmed her hip and scowled, but didn't argue anymore. Colt's smile turned genuine. "Good. Just stay here and stay quiet. I'll be back soon."

Colt set his bags down beside Dani's feet and pulled the M-4 off his shoulder. He didn't want to use it, but better to be safe than sorry. After creeping to the end of the building, he eased out just enough to catch a glimpse of the street beyond.

The soldier walked down the road, rifle perched on his shoulder, head on a slow-motion swivel. He hadn't seen them. Colt pulled back and thought about their options.

They couldn't walk into the road and make themselves known; Colt carried a stolen M-4, they both probably had a warrant out for their arrest or whatever the Guard was coming up with these days, and he couldn't explain his connection to the girl. No, that would never work.

He crept back to Dani. "The way I see it, we have two viable options. One, we wait the guy out. I don't know how long it will take or whether more guys are coming, but we could hunker down here and wait until the coast is clear and go."

She fidgeted with the zipper of her hoodie while she thought it over. "Okay. What's the other option?"

"We run for it." They had done it twice before, but never with a soldier this close.

"What if he sees us?"

Colt glanced up at the blue sky. "If we're fast, he won't."

"If we're slow?"

"Then we'll probably get caught and have to fight."

She frowned as she ran her fingernail over the tines of the zipper. "If I weren't with you, what would you do?"

Colt exhaled. "I might try to talk my way out of it. But it's too risky now. The guy I disarmed had to have made it back to the base by now. Our descriptions are all over the unit." He leaned out away from the dumpster to check the alley one more time. "If we don't try to sneak by him, we could be here all night."

"Gran will be worried sick."

"Then you're willing to try?"

"Running?" She looked up at him with eyes full of hope and determination. "You bet."

"Good." Colt reached down for his bags. "Any chance you have room in that backpack for one of these bags? They're too loud on their own."

Dani slipped her pack off her shoulders and pulled it open. Colt managed to stuff not one, but both bags inside. She hoisted it back up and onto her shoulders.

"Is it too heavy?"

"I can manage." She tightened the straps and flashed a brave smile. "Ready?"

Colt nodded. "Let's go."

Dani followed a pace behind as Colt eased around the dumpster and down the alley. As they neared the exposed edge of the building, Colt stopped. "How far to the nursing home?"

"About a mile."

"Can you get there if we separate?"

"Yes."

"All right. Then let's go. If he sees us, I want you to take off. Run as fast as you can all the way to the nursing home. If anyone follows you, try to hide."

Dani's face pinched in alarm. "What about you?"

"Just give me directions and I'll find the place."

After Dani rattled off the address and the best way to get there, Colt nodded. "Got it. Deep breath and we go on three. One, two…"

On three, the two of them took off, running in a half-crouch down the side of the building and to the street. Colt held out his hand and Dani stopped just behind him. He leaned forward and scoped out the street. The guardsman still walked straight down the middle of the road. From the distance, Colt couldn't make out anything but the green of his uniform as it stood out against the asphalt.

Could they make it across the street without being spotted? Only one way to find out.

He turned to Dani. "You go first. Run as fast and as quiet as you can across the street." He pointed at the closed copy shop ahead. "Stop at the far end of the copy store, okay?"

She nodded, but from the way her shoulders almost touched her ears, he knew she was afraid.

"I'll be right behind you. Go!"

Dani took off like a sprinter, dashing into the road. Colt raced behind her, eyes scanning in all directions.

Halfway across the pavement, Dani stumbled, but she didn't cry out. She picked herself up and kept going.

In seconds, they were across the street. Colt stopped bedside Dani and clutched the wall to catch his breath. "Good job."

"I fell."

"But you got back up." He patted her on the back. "That's what matters."

Dani smiled and it warmed Colt in a way he didn't expect. He was proud of her. As soon as the realization hit him, he shut it down. No getting attached. He couldn't stay in Eugene, and Dani couldn't leave. He'd promised to keep her safe, and he would. But as soon as he figured out what to do with her and her grandmother, Colt would be gone.

The remaining mile to the nursing home passed without incident. Other than a yowly tabby cat, they didn't pass another soul on the road. Dani pointed out the low brown building and Colt nodded. "This is it."

"Looks like a good place."

"It is."

"So how do we get in?"

Dani gave him the once over. "It's going to be a tight fit."

Five minutes later, they stood behind a row of bushes on the rear side of the facility. "There is no way I'm fitting through there."

Dani ducked beneath the cut screen and shoved the window open. "I don't know of another way in. Every door is locked and I don't have a key." She pushed it up as high as it would go before reaching for their bags. She dumped both onto the floor of the dark room and hoisted herself up and over.

Her feet landed with a thud on the other side and she stood up. "Do you want me to help pull you through?"

Colt rubbed his chin. "No. I'm going to have to do this the old-fashioned way."

"What's that?"

"Brute force. Stand back."

As Dani stepped out of the way, Colt took a deep breath and jumped. His hands landed on the sill and he managed to catapult a third of the way into the window before his shoulders stuck. "Damn it."

He wiggled his right arm, biting back a string of curse words as the metal dug into his skin, but after a moment, he pulled it free. With one arm on the inside of the window, he used his strength to push himself through the rest of the way.

Colt landed in a heap on the floor and the whole room shook.

Dani reached out her hand to help him up. "See? I knew you'd fit."

Colt mumbled his disagreement. "Let's go meet your gran."

CHAPTER TEN

DANI

Sunnyvale Convalescent Hospital
Eugene, Oregon
7:00 p.m.

"Run me through why we're stuck in this supply closet, again?"

Dani chewed on her lip while Colt expressed his distaste of her hide and lurk strategy. "Because if we get caught, the staff will kick us out."

"I'm sure if I talk to someone, I can straighten it all out. The people who are still showing up to work have to be at the end of their rope. They would welcome some relief."

Dani wasn't about to tell him about her run-in with the staff the week the grid failed or how she'd barely escaped them calling the cops. The less he knew about her life, the better. She wished she hadn't brought him to the nursing home at all.

But standing in her mom's apartment, looking at it all with a stranger's eyes…

She had never been more disgusted or ashamed. Why did she live like that? Why did she keep going back there when her mom didn't give a damn about her? *I would have been better off on the streets.*

Dani shook the thoughts off. "They aren't letting any visitors in. If a relative shows up, then the patient has to leave with them. I don't…" She twisted the cuff of her sweatshirt sleeve around her fingers. "I don't have anywhere to take Gran. She needs to stay here."

Colt didn't say anything. Did he regret rescuing her? Was he already looking for a way out? Dani didn't know anymore whether she wanted him to leave or stay. He saved her and helped her find more food and get all the way back to the nursing home without getting caught.

But could she trust him? Could she trust anyone?

At last, he broke the silence and the tornado of her thoughts. "Next time, pick a bigger closet, okay? My knees are killing me."

Dani ducked her head and smiled. "We can probably get there now. It's dark enough to sneak around."

Colt eased the door open and stuck his head into the hall. After confirming it stood empty, he let Dani take the lead. Dani didn't know how her grandmother would react to a giant guy her mom's age with a rifle slung over his shoulder, but what choice did she have?

Colt deserved to meet the woman Dani worked so

hard to protect. She sneaked a glance behind her. His square head and short hair reminded her of an action hero. The huge shoulders and ability to disarm another man only added to it. She wanted to ask him a million questions. Was he a good guy? Bad? Did he save people or hurt them or was he just a dude with a gym in his garage and too much time on his hands?

Dani would have to leave the questions to Gran. She paused outside her door. Colt didn't seem like the type to stick around, and he'd said as much, but Dani couldn't help wondering. If he stuck around long enough, maybe he'd end up being a friend.

She pushed the door open and ushered Colt through. The room was darker than the hall with the blinds drawn and she couldn't see her grandmother's bed. "Gran? Are you awake?"

Her grandmother didn't respond. Dani rushed up to the bed, leaning close enough to feel the older woman's breath on her cheek. "Gran, wake up." She gave her grandmother a gentle nudge in the shoulder.

"Are you all right?" Her grandmother whispered so faintly, Dani almost missed it.

"Yeah, of course I am." Dani pulled back. "What's with the whisper?"

Gran grabbed the edge of Dani's sweatshirt in her bony fingers but kept her eyes shut, lips barely moving as she spoke again. "That man. Is he hurting you? Are you okay?"

It took Dani a moment before it all made sense. *Oh.* She laughed and her grandmother's eyes shot open.

"Gran, I'm fine." She waved Colt over. "Colt, meet my gran."

Colt stepped up to the bed and her grandmother eyed him with distrust. "Open the blinds so I can get a better look at him."

"Do you think that's a good idea? What about the orderlies?"

Gran waved her off. "They're all gone for the day. We're fine."

Dani preferred to be cautious, but she wouldn't argue with Gran. She opened the blinds as she talked. "I swear he's not a bad guy. He saved me from a real creep of a soldier out on the road."

As Dani turned back around, Gran flicked on a flashlight she kept beside her on the bed. "Gran! Everyone will see you!"

"Hush, Dani. If you'd come back before dinner, I wouldn't need to use it. But now it's dark and my old eyes can't see. I need to get a good look at him." The beam landed square on Colt's face and he blinked. "Did you really help Danielle out there?"

"Yes, ma'am."

"You didn't kidnap my granddaughter? Force her to say these things?"

"Gran!"

"Hush, child. I want to hear him say it."

Oh my God. Her grandmother was off her rocker. Interrogating a guy twice her size who carried multiple guns and knew how to use them? What did she think she would do? Blind him with that dollar store flashlight?

Colt shielded his eyes with his hand. "Dani told you

the truth, ma'am. I helped her out of a tough situation and promised to get her back here safely."

Gran clicked the light off and Dani exhaled in relief. Anyone could have seen it from outside. What if an orderly already called the authorities? Dani watched out the window, fidgeting with her zipper while Gran adjusted the pillows behind her back. At least the interrogation was over.

Her grandmother cleared her throat. *Oh, no.*

"You're awful old to have an interest in Danielle. You aren't one of those creepy old men who likes little kids, are you?"

Dani's cheeks burned bright red. She focused on the window and refused to turn around. At least then they wouldn't see her face.

"No, ma'am. I prefer grown women for that sort of thing."

Dani almost choked on her own spit.

"Good. You can call me Dorris."

Dani turned just enough to watch Colt stick out his giant hand and give her grandmother's a quick shake.

"Thank you for rescuing Danielle."

"You're welcome."

Maybe now they could all relax.

"So what's with the rifle? Are you a hunter?"

Dani groaned. Her grandmother was going to run Colt off before he'd even sat down. "Gran, enough already."

Colt glanced her way, an unreadable expression on his face. He slipped the rifle off his shoulder and leaned it against the wall. "A soldier didn't need it. That's all."

"So you're a thief!" Gran scooted up on the bed and reached for Dani. "You go out there and get someone to take this man—"

"No!" She hated to shout, but this had all gone on long enough. "Gran, it's not like that. He took it from the guy who caught me. If Colt didn't, we wouldn't have been safe."

Her grandmother frowned, eyeing Colt from behind her wrinkled brow. "Is that true?"

"Yes, ma'am." Gran's accusation didn't seem to faze him at all. If anything, he looked amused. "To be honest, I'm more of a pistol man, myself. Never did like the M-4. Always thought it too big and hard to maneuver."

Gran eased back against her pillows. "Military, then?"

"Former Navy SEAL, ma'am. I was career until I almost lost my leg in a helo crash."

"And now?"

He scratched at his beard. "Now I'm an air marshal... Or at least I was until the planes stopped flying."

Dani turned to stare at Colt. She knew her eyes had to be round as saucers, but she couldn't help it. A Navy SEAL? No wonder the man knew how to hide and fight and get out of a jam. She shifted her weight back and forth on the balls of her feet while her grandmother peppered Colt with more questions. Where he came from, what the streets were like out there, what he knew about the power loss.

His answer stopped her cold.

"What's an EMP?"

He glanced up. "An electromagnetic pulse. I'm not a scientist, but I think it's like a really big wave of energy. It flowed through the power grid and fried it. Nothing's coming back on."

"That's crazy. The power companies have to know how to fix it."

Colt pinched the back of his neck. "According to the people I talked to, it's not fixable. Not for a long time."

Dani shook her head. "What's that mean? Weeks? Months?"

"Years. Maybe not ever."

She leaned back against the wall. "This is it? This is how we have to live now?"

Colt nodded.

Her grandmother spoke back up, asking more questions about the power and the army and what Colt thought about Eugene. Their whole conversation passed Dani by in a blur. All she could think about was life before the power went out.

At last, her grandmother turned to her with a smile. "All right. He passes."

Dani didn't even know what to say.

Gran smiled and reached out to pat her face. "Don't worry, dear. I'm just doing my job. What kind of grandmother would I be if I didn't make sure the man you brought home wasn't out to rob us or worse?"

"Not a very good one, that's for sure." Colt smiled. "It's all right, Dani. I'm glad to see your grandmother cares. After seeing where you live…"

Gran stilled and glanced at Dani. *Heck*. She'd hoped

to keep that little visit a secret. She braced herself for Gran's reaction. "I took him to Mom's place."

"Danielle!"

"I didn't know if I could trust him and I... I wanted to see if she ever came home."

Her grandmother shook her head. "I never should have let them send you back to that woman."

"You were sick. You didn't have a choice."

"I take it you and your daughter weren't on the best terms?"

Gran practically spat out her tongue. "That woman is *not* my daughter. She's Danielle's mother. Married my son, had Danielle, and a year later Ricky died at the factory in a horrible accident."

She reached for a tissue and held it up to her lips. "We couldn't even have an open casket. But that woman... She blew through the insurance money like it grew on a tree in the backyard... Shacked up with I don't know how many men... Got hooked on those drugs and then—"

"Gran, that's enough." Dani hated it when her grandmother went on a tear about her mom, but to have Colt stand there like a ghost and listen to the whole thing... She shook her head. "You know she didn't get addicted on purpose. She hurt her back. The pain pills the doctor gave her were too much. She couldn't get off them. When he stopped writing her the prescription... that's when everything went downhill."

"*Hmph.* That's what her lawyer said, but I don't believe it."

"I do." Dani reached for her grandmother's hand

and gave it a squeeze. "She wouldn't have let things get so bad if she hadn't taken those pills, Gran. I know it."

Her grandmother exhaled. "You were a little girl, Dani. You didn't see the whole picture."

"I saw enough." Dani pulled away from her grandmother and bent to open her backpack. She held out Colt's two shopping bags without looking up and he took them from her hands.

Bringing Colt to visit Gran had been a mistake. Now she'd poisoned him against her mother and told secrets she had no right to tell. Dani kept her head down as her grandmother's tirade rattled around in her head like marbles in a tin can.

She needed some air. "I'm going to check out the floor. See if anyone's still on shift."

"Danielle, are you sure that's a good idea?"

She stood up and brushed off Gran's concern. "Yeah. I'm sure. I'll be back in a while. There's some food in the backpack."

Colt spoke up. "I'll make sure she eats."

"Thanks." Dani rushed out of the room before either of them could see her cry.

CHAPTER ELEVEN

COLT

Sunnyvale Convalescent Hospital
Eugene, Oregon
7:30 p.m.

Colt pulled up a chair next to the old woman's bed and sat down. His feet ached from a day on the hot asphalt and his back cramped up from the tumble in from the too-small window, but the company pleasantly surprised him.

After grilling him a bit harder once Dani left the room, her grandmother seemed to accept he wasn't interested in anything more than helping the pair of them for a little while. He slipped his hands behind his head and leaned back.

"What was Dani's father like?"

Dorris smiled at the memory. "A good man. My son worked fourteen-hour days to take care of that little baby." Her smile faded as she glanced at Colt. "He never should have married Becky. That woman was trouble from the start."

"Dani's mom?"

Dorris nodded. "All she ever saw in him was a meal ticket. A good factory job, health care. That's all my Ricky was to her. If she hadn't gotten pregnant, I'd have been able to talk some sense into him."

Colt bit back a smile. Mothers never approved of the people their kids dated, but it sounded like Dorris might have been right this time. "Dani said she hurt her back?"

"A few months after Ricky died, Becky was in a nasty car accident. A postal service van ran a red light and T-boned her. Wrapped the little Honda around a telephone pole."

"Sounds like she was lucky to be alive."

Dorris snorted. "Would have been better if she died. It took me three years to get that baby away from her. Three years of pills then pot then meth. Every man she brought home was worse than the last. The one she was with when everything went to hell, Lord have mercy, I thought he was gonna kill her and Dani too."

Colt knew guys in the service who couldn't get off their pain pills. Doctors were willing to write anyone a prescription these days for a narcotic. Thirty on oxy and good luck trying to kick the habit. He'd seen it so many times that Colt vowed never to touch the stuff. He didn't even take aspirin anymore.

Part of him didn't want to drag painful memories out of Dorris, but he needed to know what he was getting into. Assessing risk was the only way to stay alive when the world went to shit. "What happened to the last guy?"

"He had Becky all strung out, begging for another hit. She tried to—" Dorris coughed, choking on her own words, and Colt rose up to stand. She waved him off with a crumpled tissue in her hand. "When he wouldn't give her any more drugs, Becky tried to sell Dani to him, but he said she was too young. That he needed her at least seven." Dorris trembled on the bed and the sheets rustled around her. "*Seven.*"

Colt hung his head. He'd seen some terrible things in his years of active duty, but kids like Dani always got to him. "What did she do?"

"Becky stole. Got caught trying to rob a convenience store. She had a knife, no gun, but they charged her with armed robbery. She didn't get out until Dani was ten and by then, she'd been living with me for so long, that the court let her stay. If I hadn't gotten sick…"

"Cancer, right?"

Dorris nodded.

Colt hated to ask, but he pressed on. "Is it in remission?"

She stayed silent for a moment, staring at him. Her wrinkled skin pinched around her lips. "It was for a while, but it came back earlier this year." Dorris glanced up at the door. "Don't tell Dani, she doesn't know."

"How bad?"

Dorris smiled. "I won't be leaving this bed even if the whole building falls down around me."

Colt nodded. The minute he'd seen her frail body,

propped up on pillows to seem larger and more substantial, he'd known. Her skin hung on her bones like a ninety-five-year-old, loose and crepe paper thin. A breeze would knock her over.

Dorris was holding on for Dani, but there would come a time when she wouldn't wake up. He wondered how Dani would survive when her grandmother was gone. He dropped his voice a bit lower. "Do you know how she's been living these last few years?"

Dorris closed her eyes. "Not well."

"It doesn't seem like it."

"When she stopped coming to visit, I feared the worst. But I'm an old woman who can't walk more than five steps at a time. I couldn't help her."

Colt spared Dorris the details. The woman had enough guilt heaped on her hunched shoulders, she didn't need any more. He pushed himself up to stand. "If it's all right with you, I'm going to find an empty room and get some sleep."

Dorris nodded. "That's what Dani does, too. Will you be here in the morning?"

"Yes, ma'am."

The old woman smiled and beneath the wrinkles and the pain, he could see her beauty. She'd been a stunner, once. "Sleep well, Colt."

"You too, Dorris."

He grabbed his things and eased the door open. The place managed to stay cool at night thanks to the drop in temperature outside, but Colt wondered how long the facility could keep going. Whatever fuel source they were using to keep the critical patients alive, it had to run out soon. Dorris told him the orderlies came to her room once a day with a bucket of water and flushed the toilet.

They were still working, but for how long? That any staff showed up at all amazed Colt. If the place kept going much longer, other people would notice. People who lacked the same moral framework as Colt. People who wanted the path of least resistance.

Maybe Eugene was one of those towns that would escape the worst of the fallout and rebuild quickly, but Colt didn't know. From what he'd seen, only portions of the college and this little nursing home had power. If the army really had figured out how to use nearby wind turbines, then the power they supplied along with the string of port-a-potties outside the stadium could keep the army going for a long time.

What about everyone else? Would the National Guard turn the stadium into a camp? Would everyone from town be rounded up and turned into cattle? If that happened, Dani could say goodbye to Dorris. Dani would be processed, assigned a number and a cot and given an MRE a day to survive.

What would happen after that? What would happen to her when the aid ran out? He'd seen it in Haiti and Africa. Aid would flood the area in the beginning, bringing water and tents and a bunch of shiny new supplies.

But a month later? The water source would be spreading disease, the tents would be cesspools of filth, and the aid workers would be gone. On to the next crisis. The victims would be worse off than before anyone showed up.

Colt shook his head. The National Guard might be the only reason the town hadn't descended into chaos. But why were they there? What was the point?

Even after two weeks of living in the confines of the university dorms, he didn't have any answers. Sure, a few of the soldiers had shared some rumors: cities burned nationwide and the president hiding underground. But what did it mean for the future of the country? Who was leading this unit? Where were the orders coming from?

Colt wouldn't sleep easy until he left Eugene, Oregon far, far behind.

As he walked down the hall, he peered into every room, checking to see if he could claim one as his own. He found Dani four doors away.

She slept on the bed, curled up in a tight little ball, looking every bit the little girl. Her arms wrapped around something soft and furry. A stuffed animal?

Colt ached for her. The hell she'd been through in only fifteen years. Tomorrow he would get up and take her out of the nursing home and show her a few things to survive. When he left, he wanted Dani to be prepared to make it on her own.

He didn't think Dorris would last too much longer.

DAY SEVENTEEN

CHAPTER TWELVE

COLT

Downtown
    Eugene, Oregon
    6:00 a.m.

"I don't understand why we're here. It's not like we need printer paper." Dani stood with her back to Colt, on lookout.

"No one's thought to break in yet. These places have tons of stuff we can use." *Things that might get you through while I'm gone.* Colt kept the last bit to himself. He'd been crouched in front of the rear door to the office supply store for at least ten minutes, fiddling with the lock.

He hated doing things the hard way, but there hadn't been another way in and if he wanted to keep their find a secret, he needed to be tidy.

And a hell of a lot faster.

With a deep breath he went back to work, holding down the one little screwdriver while he jammed the other one in the lock. At least the nursing home had plenty of random tools like eyeglass kits. He'd been able to pilfer a couple tiny screwdrivers without any trouble.

They worked better than paper clips, but picking a commercial lock was a slow process. One that required more patience than Colt usually possessed. But Dani would need access to food and water and anything else they could find. He couldn't leave her with nothing.

After another few minutes of agonizing scraping, the lock finally clicked. "Bingo."

"Took you long enough. I thought you were supposed to be an expert or something."

"Not at this. Give me a nighttime assault on a compound just off the coast and I'm your guy. Picking the lock of a store in the States? Not so much." He pulled the door open and held it wide. "After you."

Dani ducked inside the dark store and Colt followed, making sure to lock it again immediately. As long as they kept their light use to a minimum, they should be able to case the place uninterrupted.

"Now what?" Dani stood beside Colt, her thumbs tucked into her pockets, waiting.

"We raid."

Colt headed straight toward the rear of the store, eyes constantly scanning for a hidden threat. Breaking into an office store wasn't the same as urban warfare—not by a long shot—but the premise was the same. Get in, secure the target, get out. That's all they were doing today.

Dani stayed close to his heels, never more than a step or two behind. At the far wall he stopped and flicked on a flashlight. "What do you see?"

She glanced up at the wall. "A bunch of cleaning supplies."

"Look harder." Colt waited while Dani stared straight ahead. The second she saw it, she smiled. "First aid kits."

"Good. What else?"

"Hand sanitizer. Wipes." She rushed over to the next shelving area past a section of clearance stickers. "Toilet paper and paper towels and cups and silverware." She turned to him. "How did you know all of this would be here?"

"I'm observant." He motioned toward the middle of the store. "Let's go find some backpacks and we can put a few things together."

Twenty minutes later, they had backpacks filled with first aid kits and sanitizer. Dani could barely zip hers shut. "I wish this place sold luggage."

Colt hadn't thought of it before, but Dani had a good point. "They do, sort of. Come on." He found the aisle after a few minutes of searching. "Grab one of those, we can find a box cutter in the packing supplies to get it open."

Dani pulled a black hunk of plastic off the shelf as Colt retraced his steps to the packing supplies. He grabbed a couple rolls of duct tape and two box cutters before heading back. With a few swipes of the knife, he cut the zip ties keeping the black crate flat and popped it open.

Dani nodded in recognition. "One of my teachers used to have something like this. She would wheel it in full of supplies or graded papers every Monday morning."

Colt nodded. "They'll come in handy for transporting water."

"The nursing home has water. Why would we need any more?"

"At some point it's going to run out and you'll need to find some on your own. This store has a ton."

"I saw the refrigerated cases up front, but there can't be more than fifty bottles between them."

"Not those." Colt led Dani to the other corner of the store and stopped in front of the office cooler section. "Fifteen five-gallon water containers right here. That's enough water for one person for two and a half months. Longer if you conserve."

Dani stared up in wonder and Colt couldn't help but smile. It didn't take much to impress the kid, but he gave himself a small pat on the back all the same. If even a portion of all he showed her sank in, she might have a chance to make it after he left.

"Do you really think we should be doing this?"

"What?"

Dani hesitated. "Stealing."

Colt wondered if she would ever ask. "I don't have a good answer, to be honest. At some point, it comes down to survival. Would you rather steal and survive or not and die?"

"Survive." She said it with so much conviction in her slight voice.

"Then we don't have a choice." He flicked off his light and the pair of them stood in semidarkness, the only light coming in from the morning sun outside. "Do you have a lot of friends here in Eugene?"

Dani jerked at the question. "Not really." She glanced at the floor. "I had a few at the old school when I lived with Gran, but once I moved back in with my mom... None of the kids really liked me at the new one."

Colt nodded. "That's good."

"It is?" She lifted her head, confusion marring her young brow. "How is being a loner good?"

"It means you're already a survivor. If you can handle going to school everyday where no one likes you, then you can survive when food and water are scarce and you can't trust anyone."

He could see her thinking over the idea that she was somehow more prepared for this new world than the popular girls who probably shunned her. Colt hoped it gave her courage and strength. The girl would need it.

"Let's go see what food they have up front. I saw a bunch of trail mix and some Slim Jims."

Dani groaned. "I thought Twinkies would be the thing that survived after all the people died, but I was wrong. It'll be Slim Jims."

Colt laughed. "I take it you're not a fan."

Dani shook her head. "Have you eaten three or four in a row?" When he shook his head, she made a gross face. "Don't or you'll be stinking up the place for days."

"Only one Slim Jim per meal. Got it."

Dani laughed and the pair of them walked toward

the front of the store, each one with a backpack stuffed full of supplies and a rolling cart with a five-gallon bottle of water inside. When they reached the front, Dani paused. "What about flashlights?"

She pointed at a display of little LED flashlights and batteries and Colt nodded. "Definitely. Good catch." They opened a few packages and tested which gave off the brightest beam before adding them to their stash.

"Now grab as many packages of nuts as you can fit in your pack and let's get out of here."

Dani did as Colt instructed, grabbing bags of pecans and pistachios and shoving them into every little crevice of her backpack. "If we know this place is here, why bother taking more than we need? We can always come back."

"We don't know that for sure. The National Guard could mobilize tomorrow and demand everyone move to the university campus or someone else could find this place and do a smash and grab. There's so much uncertainty out here now, it's always better to be prepared."

Colt didn't elaborate on all the potential pitfalls that awaited a girl like Dani. She was so young to be out on her own with no one to protect her. He frowned. "Do you know how to use a gun?"

Her eyes went wide as she glanced up at his face. "No."

"Then I should teach you. I don't know how easy it will be to find you a weapon around here, but that should be one of the first things we do. The more prepared you are to defend yourself the better."

"You make it sound like it's the Wild West out there, but I haven't seen any of that. Those military guys seemed to be all over the place. No one is going to try anything with them around."

Colt exhaled. The more he thought about the military presence in the little town, the more it didn't make sense. Whatever they were doing there, it couldn't just be law and order. There were other places that needed the help more.

All the more reason to get out of Eugene as quickly as possible. "Come on, let's get out of here before we run into one of them."

Colt and Dani wheeled their carts to the back door and after he unlocked it, they both slipped outside. Colt crouched and shoved a shim beneath the door. It wouldn't keep many people out, but at least he'd know if someone else found the place.

As he stood up, he realized Dani had gone on without him. *Shit.* She should have known by now not to leave first. What was she thinking? Colt hustled to the end of the store, but froze when a voice cut the silence.

"Well lookie what we've got here, boys. *Mmm.* I bet you clean up real nice."

Oh, no. Colt eased the cart back to an upright position and slipped his backpack off his shoulders. He unholstered the Sig and checked to ensure it was ready to fire. With a deep breath, he calmed his nerves and found that place he always went to right before a battle.

Whatever predator was out there talking to Dani wouldn't leave the area alive.

CHAPTER THIRTEEN

DANI

DOWNTOWN
Eugene, Oregon
7:30 a.m.

OH, CRAP. DANI STOOD FROZEN IN PLACE, TOO AFRAID to move a muscle. Four men loitered in front of her, all looking like the sort of guy her mother liked to date. The one who spoke to her stroked his goatee, rubbing his fingers down his chin and leering.

They all wore black vests, and from the look of them had to be in a gang. Dani had seen them before in the area her mom lived, riding massive bikes with those crazy handlebars that stretched toward the sky. A motorcycle club, her mother called them.

Her mother had been fascinated by them, thought maybe they would take care of her and keep her high. The only time her mom went out with one, she'd come home with a black eye and an empty wallet. That incident told Dani all she needed to know about the men in front of her. They were bad and all staring at her like she would be their next meal.

One on the far left stepped forward. He carried a baseball bat in his right hand and as he walked, he swung it in an arc. "How about you wheel that cart over here and let me get a better look at you? Jimmy thinks you're a fine piece, but I'm on the fence. I don't do scrawny girls and you look kinda scrawny to me."

I should have waited for Colt. Thoughts of the man who'd saved her once already gave her hope. He had to be coming, didn't he? He wouldn't leave her there in the middle of the road to fend off these thugs alone.

Dani tugged her sweatshirt closer around her body.

"Aw, looks like she ain't gonna do what you want, Steve. Whatcha gonna do 'bout it, huh?"

The guy named Steve sneered at the one who'd called him out. "Shut up, Jimmy." A scar ran across his cheek and into his upper lip and every time he spoke, it curved like a sick grin. He swung the bat again.

One of the guys holding back spoke up. "Let's just take her loot and go. Those army guys gotta be headed this way." He wore his hair cut short and his black vest looked newer than the others. A new recruit, maybe. Not that it mattered. Even if he stood on the sidelines, Dani couldn't get away from four of them.

She glanced behind her. Colt wasn't anywhere to be found.

"Aw, you tryin' to find a place to hide, baby?" Jimmy stepped forward, stopping when he stood next to Steve.

"Don't you know you can't run from the Ryder MC? We're all over these streets. And we get what we ask for." He grabbed his crotch and Dani looked away.

A chill rushed through her despite the sun. *I have to run*. She swallowed and pushed the rolling basket in front of her. "Here, you can have this."

"Aw, ain't she sweet." Jimmy put his hand over his heart and mock-swooned. "Givin' me her water like it's what I wanted." His smile slipped into a sneer. "It ain't what I want girlie, and you know it. Now get your ass over here and give me a kiss."

Dani's fingers shook and heart beat so loud she didn't know how no one else heard it. Jimmy took another step toward her and that was it. Something inside Dani snapped. Snapshot memories popped into her mind. Greasy palms and dirty hair. Rough fingers and violent words. Tin foil burning and her mom's scratchy laugh.

No one awake to tuck her in or read her a story. No one who cared enough to feed her dinner or wash her hair. She'd been so little.

Fear smothered her like a wet blanket. She knew she needed to run, but her feet stuck to the asphalt like they'd been baked into it. Where was Colt when she needed him? Why wasn't he coming to her rescue?

She'd survived these past few years with her mom by making herself scarce whenever the drugs came out. The fire escape had been her safety net. Every knock on the door meant Dani had thirty seconds to run. She'd gotten good at predicting the type of man by the way his knuckles hit the wood.

Hard meant a hothead. Insistent, a drug addict. Soft was dangerous and Dani had to run like hell. These men were dangerous and her time was running out.

Dani dropped the handle on the cart and turned to run, but the backpack weighed her down. She made it ten feet before Steve with the bat caught up to her. His fist closed around her hair and he yanked her back like a yo-yo at the end of its string.

Her body kept going while her head jerked and in seconds, she was flying, feet off the ground, body in mid-air. The ground rose up to meet her and she hit hard on her butt, slamming into the asphalt as Steve held her head a few feet off the ground.

"I told you I wanted a closer look." He reached down and grabbed the hem of her sweatshirt, but Dani struggled, kicking and lashing out with her fists. Her foot collided with his arm and Steve cursed.

When the bat hit her ribs, she stopped fighting.

CHAPTER FOURTEEN

COLT

Downtown
  Eugene, Oregon
  7:39 a.m.

THE SECOND THE ASSHOLE SWUNG THE BAT, COLT sprang into action. He'd been waiting, watching, and hoping Dani would get far enough away that he could drop the SOBs where they stood. But she froze, instead.

Colt understood. Lots of people in Dani's position would do the same thing. But he'd hoped she would have been more of a fighter. She could still learn. As soon as he took care of the wannabe motorcycle crew, he'd teach her to stand up for herself and the best time to run.

Colt stepped out from behind the building and aimed at the closest man. "Tell your friend to let the girl go, or you'll be dead before your body hits the pavement."

Everyone looked up. Four men without a conscience among them. Steve, the one holding Dani by the hair, hauled her up to her feet. "I see you've got an admirer. Someone else who wants to see what you've got hiding under all those clothes."

He reached for her waist and Colt took aim. The trigger pulled like a knife through hot butter and the man next to Steve crumpled to the ground. One round between the eyes. DOA.

Colt cocked his head. "Did you not hear me the first time? I said let her go."

Steve pulled Dani close, using her as a shield. "You'll never be able to hit me. Not with her in the way."

Colt resisted the urge to roll his eyes. "Just wait." Colt fired again, shooting the one called Jimmy smack in the chest. As the man sagged to his knees, Colt shot again for good measure.

That left the silent one in the back and Steve to go. The man who hadn't said a word stared at Colt for a moment before turning to run. Poor bastard didn't even have his name tape on the back of his vest, he was so new. Picked the wrong crowd, buddy.

Colt thought about shooting him in the back as he ran, then thought better of it. The scared MC member darted around a building and disappeared.

"Looks like it's just you and me now, Steve. How about you let the girl go?"

Steve's eyes were wild and uncontrolled, darting this way and that, first at his dead friends and then at Colt.

"We just wanted to have a little fun, man. That's all. Just a little fun."

Colt advanced on the guy, all the while waiting for a clean shot. "No. You wanted to rape an innocent girl. She's only a kid. You should pick on someone your own size."

Dani stood in front of Steve, not struggling, maybe not even breathing. She stared at Colt with a mix of terror and determination. She might have failed to get away, but she wasn't a blubbering mess, begging Colt to save her.

If only she would get out of the way.

He would have to distract Steve enough to give Dani a chance. Shooting her on accident wasn't going to happen. He'd rather let Steve take her and chase him down instead of risking killing the kid. He glanced up at Steve.

The man still held Dani by the hair, the brown strands looped around his hand to form a painful bridle. In his other hand, he still held the bat. It swung back and forth every time Steve turned to look at his dead friends.

Colt only had one option.

Air marshals were some of the best shots in the world. The government didn't trust just anyone to fire a bullet inside a pressured metal cylinder flying at attitude. One wrong shot a few miles high, and the bad guy wouldn't be the only person dying on a plane.

He took aim and the world slowed. His breath sawed into his lungs like a bellow filling with air. His heart beat low and long like a gong underwater. His vision tunneled and all he saw were the sights and the target.

Colt fired and Steve's hand holding the bat practically exploded.

The man screamed, loosened his grip on Dani, and she ran. A tortured yell ripped from her throat as a massive clump of her hair tore off her head and she stumbled, but it didn't matter. She was free.

Colt didn't waste any time. He fired again and Steve fell to the ground with his friends.

Dani ran up to Colt, tears leaving streaks down her dirty face. She crushed against his chest, thick sobs muffled by his shirt. She tried to speak, but he couldn't understand a thing. Now wasn't the time to have a heart-to-heart.

Someone, somewhere, heard those shots. They might be on the middle of a street full of closed-up shops, but there were houses and apartments not that far away. The National Guard patrolled on the regular. That no one else appeared in the street while it had all gone down was a miracle.

Eugene might be quiet, but it wasn't empty. They had minutes at best. He reached down and pulled Dani far enough away to look her in the eye. "Can you run?"

She blinked through the fear and relief. "I-I think so."

"Good. Grab your things. We need to disappear."

The sound of a truck horn in the distance shocked Dani into action. She ran for her backpack and tugged it back on before grabbing the cart with water.

"Leave the water!"

"What? No!"

"It's not worth your life." Colt grabbed her by the hand. "Let's go. We'll grab my bag on the way."

He didn't know if they would outrun the rig headed their way, but they would have to try.

CHAPTER FIFTEEN

DANI

IF ONLY THE SHAKES WOULD GO AWAY. DANI TWISTED her hands around each other and tried to force her limbs to stay still. It didn't work. Now her whole body trembled.

During the entire escape from the four men in the street, adrenaline kept Dani going. Faster, faster they ran, through alleys and backyards, at least a mile away from the scene of the crime. No matter how she looked at it, she couldn't escape it. Colt killed those four men and Dani wasn't sad about it.

Did that make her a monster? Was this how it would be from now on? Kill or be killed? She'd been sheltered inside the nursing home, pretending the outside world wasn't falling to pieces, slowly becoming more and more like the world her mother lived in all the time.

Now she sat in a looted pharmacy, hiding behind the counter while Colt searched for supplies. A moment later, he eased around a toppled-over shelving unit with his hands full and came to crouch beside her. "Turn this way so I can get a look at your head."

"I... It's fine."

"Nonsense. You're bleeding. Turn around."

Dani begrudgingly complied, twisting until Colt could get a good look at the new bald spot in the middle of her scalp. She winced as he dabbed it with antiseptic. "How bad is it?"

"You lost a good bit of hair and some skin, but it should heal up no problem." He hesitated. "But I don't know if you'll ever regrow the hair."

It could have been worse. "Thank you for what you did back there." She couldn't bring herself to say killing those men, although she was grateful for it.

"You're welcome. I'm sorry I didn't get to you sooner."

"It's okay. I'm just thankful you came at all."

Colt grabbed her by the shoulders and spun her around. The look in his eyes turned her throat to sandpaper. "Dani, I promised you that I would protect you, and as long as I'm around, that's what I'm going to do. Like I said before, I'd be a terrible dad, but I know how to kill people. That's one thing I'm good at."

"You're a better dad than I've ever had." As soon as she said the words, she wished she could take them back. Colt let her go like she'd burned him. She rushed to fill the silence. "I'm sorry, I shouldn't have said that. I don't know what I was thinking."

He stood up in an awkward rush. "It's all right. I'm going to poke around the place. See if I can find any medicine to take with us. There's still a few bottles here and there."

Dani bit her lip hard enough to hurt. She knew Colt didn't want to stay. She could tell in the way he always kept himself a bit apart, how he never talked about what he would do more than a day in the future. No matter how hard Dani tried to hold onto him, Colt would leave.

Just like everyone did.

While Colt busied himself searching the wreckage of the pharmacy, Dani thought about the past twenty-four hours. She'd been caught stealing food by a National Guardsman, rescued by a badass who then insisted on being her shadow for the rest of the day, took him not only to see the roach-infested hell hole she'd been living in, but then to meet her grandmother.

No wonder the man wanted to get away.

Today, when he'd tried to help her gather supplies she almost got herself kidnapped. Colt had not only saved her, he'd killed for her. She would never be able to repay him. Maybe leaving would be the best thing for him. How many times would she need saving? How many times would he be able to protect her before their luck ran out?

He traipsed back into the alcove where she sat, a huge grin on his face. "Cipro and Z-Pak. How lucky is that?"

Dani stared up at him blankly.

"Shelf-stable antibiotics. They'll both last at least five years if we keep them out of the sun."

There were so many things she didn't know. "Any chance you found some Advil back there?"

Colt winced. "No, sorry. But I bet your grandmother will have some."

Gran. She was probably taking her mid-morning nap, oblivious to the danger her granddaughter kept finding around every corner. "Right. So are we headed back there now?"

Colt stuffed the antibiotics in his pack and crouched back down to look her in the eye. "We're far enough away from the scene that we should be fine if anyone stops us."

"You mean the National Guard?"

Colt nodded. "They'll assume some rival gang took them out, not a kid and an old man."

Dani hid most of a smile. He wasn't *that* old. "What do you want to do?"

"First, we're going to find you an apartment."

"What?" She must have misheard him.

Colt smiled. "There have to be tons of empty apartments near the nursing home. It's so close to the campus, lots of places probably rent to students. Most of them left town the second the power went out. The whole university is like a ghost town. Apart from the people I knew there, it's basically all military at this point."

Dani still didn't get where he was going. "So?"

"So there will be a bunch of off-campus apartments

full of furniture with no one to live in them. You're going to pick one."

She raised an eyebrow. "I'm going to live in my own apartment?"

"Beats the hell out of a spare bed in a nursing home, don't you think?"

Dani let a full smile shine. "Yes, it does."

* * *

52 HOUGHTON STREET, APARTMENT 310
Eugene, Oregon
2:00 p.m.

"ARE YOU SURE? IT'S AWFULLY BIG." DANI SPUN around the living room, taking in the view from the corner windows. She could see almost all of the college campus and the nursing home and a few blocks beyond.

"It's perfect. All the windows mean tons of natural light. It's got good vantage points, and the building is still secure. The place looks mostly empty, so you won't have to worry about people outing you as a squatter."

Colt walked over to the front door and gave it a thud. "The metal door means you can stay safe. Between that and the concrete walls, you could probably even ride out a fire inside the building."

Dani never thought the end of the modern world would give her a loft apartment overlooking a ton of town, but she wasn't complaining. "You're sure we can do this?"

"Yes. I've been through the desk and the mail by the front door. It's a student's place. She's from Southern California. I'm sure she took the first chance she could to go home. There's no food in the fridge and it looks like she took her cat. She's not coming back."

"Okay. Then, I guess I'll stay." She shouldn't ask, but she couldn't help herself. "What about you?"

Colt shrugged. "I figured I could sleep on the couch until you got comfortable. A few days, maybe."

"And then?"

He voiced the words she hoped she wouldn't hear. "Then I'll be moving on."

"Right. Okay." Dani flashed him a fake smile and turned back to the windows. She wouldn't let her disappointment show. Colt had done so much for her already. The least she could do was be grateful. If he wanted to leave, she wouldn't get in his way.

With this new place and more food and supplies, she could make it on her own. Dani turned back around and exhaled. "So what do we do now?"

"Now we clear some space in the living room and I teach you how to fight."

CHAPTER SIXTEEN

COLT

52 HOUGHTON STREET, APARTMENT 310
Eugene, Oregon
5:00 p.m.

DANI DODGED THE SOFT PUNCH COLT DIRECTED
toward her jaw and Colt smiled. "Good. You're getting
the hang of it."

She palmed her hips while sucking in a lungful of
air. "You really think so?"

"Definitely. With a little more practice, next time
you'll be able to handle yourself."

With her hair pulled back in a ponytail and her
ragged sweatshirt tossed on the chair, Dani looked far
younger than fifteen. If Colt had been a guessing man,
he'd have said twelve. Mostly skin and bones, the poor
girl looked like she hadn't had a good meal ever since
her grandmother got sick.

What she lacked in muscles and strength, she made up for with innate smarts. She couldn't fight someone Colt's size and win, but she knew how to bob and weave and how to evade. If she could master the maneuvers he showed her that afternoon, she stood a chance out there. Even if he left.

"Now we're onto attack." Colt stepped up to Dani's side and grabbed her hand. "When someone comes at you, what advantages do you have?"

Her brown eyes flitted to the ceiling as she thought it over. "I'm small, so I can get away?"

"That's one. But you're also fast." He spun around to face her. "Say I'm coming at you and you can't outrun me. What can you do?"

"Scream?"

"What else?"

"Kick or punch?"

"Better. But your punches won't faze a guy like me."

She screwed up her face and Colt grinned. "I'm over two hundred pounds, Dani."

Her mouth fell open. "You are?"

"Yep. To your fist, I'd be a slab of concrete. That's why you have to go for the softer areas. Eyes. Groin. Feet."

"Your feet?"

Colt nodded. "As soon as we can, we need to hit a sporting goods store and get you some good boots with a steel toe and a lug sole. If you stomp on someone in those, you can break their toes."

Dani glanced down at her faded, dirty sneakers. "Or I could kick you where it hurts."

Now she was catching on. "Exactly. You aim a solid kick with a steel toe to a guy's family jewels and he'll be rolling on the ground calling for his momma."

"What about eyes? That sounds gross."

"It is. But if someone gets a hold of you like Steve did," Colt rushed up to her and wrapped his arm around her throat, dragging her back until her body fell against his. Dani fought, but couldn't get away. "Instead of squirming and fighting, what can you do?"

She tentatively reached up over her head and felt Colt's face. "Gouge your eyes out?"

"Bingo." He let her go and waited for her to turn around. "If your hands are free, take your index and middle finger together and hold them straight out like a spear. Then jab as hard as you can right into his eye."

Dani's mouth turned down and looked a bit green. "I don't know if I can do that."

"If it's pop someone's eyeball or be tortured and killed, which would you rather?"

She exhaled. "Eyeball popping."

"You're damn right. I'm not saying it won't be hard. Fighting back is the hardest thing you'll have to do." Colt had seen it so many times. Innocent people who weren't conditioned in hand-to-hand combat never wanted to be aggressive. "It's easy to stand still and let someone hurt you. It's hard to take a stand. But that's what you have to do to survive."

Dani nodded, but her eyes seemed far away. After a moment, she spoke up. "Have you done a lot of this? Hand-to-hand combat?"

"More than I'd like. But it's necessary in times of

war. And that's sort of what we're in, Dani. The military might be out there now, patrolling the streets, but at some point, they'll leave. When the law enforcement is gone, this town will fall back on its Wild West roots. It'll be every person for themselves."

"What if I try all of these things and it doesn't work? I still get captured."

Colt ran his fingers over his lips. He didn't want to tell her the truth. That she might wish for the day her heart stopped beating just for the pain and horror to end. He'd known a prisoner of war. The stories he told...

Colt cleared his throat. "Never give up hope. If you're always looking for a way out, you'll find one. Some way, somehow, you'll find an opening. It might not happen right away. It might take longer than you imagined, but if you keep searching, you'll find it."

"Never give up. That's what you're saying."

"The second you do, you might as well be dead."

Dani nodded. "I can do that. The last few years with my mom... they weren't easy. But I always kept my eyes and ears open. It was how I managed."

"Then if the unthinkable happens, fall back on those skills. At some point, you'll find a weakness and exploit it."

Dani glanced past Colt toward the kitchen. "Any chance your current weakness involves dinner? I'm starved."

Colt agreed and let Dani lead the way into the kitchen. She opened the cabinets one by one, standing up on her tiptoes to see into the back. It had only been a couple days, but Colt was really growing to like the girl. Never in a million years did he ever think he would get some bug to be a dad. It wasn't in the cards for a Navy SEAL or an air marshal.

Too dangerous and too many missions and trips overseas. Colt always said if he couldn't do something 110 percent, then he wouldn't do it. Parenting, relationships, his job. The same. So he'd ended up giving it all to the job. Maybe that had been the wrong call.

Dani pulled down a box of crackers, a can of tuna, and bag of sunflower seeds. She waved them in Colt's direction. "It's five-star cuisine tonight."

His stomach growled and she laughed.

Maybe he didn't need to leave. While Dani fished around in the drawers for a can opener, Colt made himself busy finding plates and napkins. They might not have a dishwasher or running water, but they could still eat on a plate.

Dani deserved a chance to grow up protected and cared for. He never wanted to be a father, and he wouldn't have wished for this circumstance in a million years, but people change. Maybe now was his time. Maybe this was his chance to experience a different sort of life. One without airplanes and threats and bad guys halfway around the world.

There were plenty of bad guys right here in this small college town. He could protect Dani and help her grow up. Give her a glimpse of a grownup who cared.

"Finally!" She pulled out a manual can opener, her brown eyes shining in the evening light. As Dani opened the can of tuna, Colt pulled out the crackers. He piled a handful on each plate and divided the seeds in half.

Dani scooped the fish onto the plates and they carried everything over to the little table tucked against the wall. She sat down and took a look around. "You're sure we can do this? Just stay here and use all these things?"

Colt leaned back in his chair. "For now, yes. If the girl who lives here comes back, we can apologize and leave. But I don't think she's coming back. Without airplanes or running gas stations, how far is anyone going to get."

"I've seen some cars on the road. More over by my mom's place."

"It's been over two weeks. The college kids are long gone. After the college told them to leave, they did. Everyone else in town had to hear the same announcements. If they had family somewhere, I'm sure a lot of people left."

Dani shoveled a bite of tuna into her mouth with a cracker. "But what about the police?"

"I haven't seen any, have you?"

She shook her head. "Not since the National Guard rolled in."

"Then I think we're fine. But that's something you need to keep in mind. We may need to leave at a moment's notice. You should always be prepared to walk away."

Dani stilled. "I can't leave Gran."

Right. Her grandmother. If he hadn't promised the old woman not to tell Dani about the cancer, he would have done so already. She deserved to know the truth. But he couldn't break the confidence of a dying woman.

Colt scooped up some of the fish and topped it with some seeds before shoving it all and a cracker into his mouth. "*Mmm*. You're ready for *Top Chef*, you know that?"

She smiled. "When I lived with Gran we watched so much TV."

"Really? I'm surprised she didn't say it would rot your brain."

"Oh, she did. That's why there were rules. Cooking, gardening, nature shows. I could watch all of those I wanted." She scooped up some sunflower seeds and took a bite, swallowing it down with a gulp of water. "*The X-Files* was the only show I could watch that didn't have to be true."

Colt almost dropped his tuna-laden cracker. "*The X-Files?*"

Dani's eyes almost sparkled. "I've seen every episode at least twice. Gran had a thing for Mulder."

"I've seen them all, too. I can't believe your gran and I have something in common."

Dani paused. "You're into Mulder, too?"

Colt laughed out loud. "No! But his partner? Hell, yes." He shook his head. "Redheads, man. They're nothing but trouble."

Dani laughed and it warmed Colt like a familiar song on the radio. Something he'd missed these past weeks. Radio. TV. All the things people used to escape into, gone. Now they only had each other to fill that void. He wished he'd known Dani before the power grid failed. He could have saved her from so much pain.

She might be smiling now, but it had been difficult to get here. They ate with relish, diving into the fish and crackers like it was a juicy burger at Colt's favorite bar back home. All the while, they laughed and talked, Dani explaining about her favorite books and Colt sharing a little about his life as an air marshal.

After they finished, Colt stood up with a sigh. "It's getting dark. We should head back to the nursing home and check on your grandmother before curfew sets in."

Dani reached for his plate. "Let's clean these up and we can go."

Ten minutes later, they were once again walking down the street in Eugene, eyes open and ears listening. It was quiet that night; not even the sound of birds or crickets broke the stillness. They eased into the nursing home through the same window as before and this time Colt managed to not fall on his backside squeezing through.

They walked down the hall, both light on their feet, smiles on their faces. The place was deserted.

Dani leaned into Colt's side. "Just wait until I tell Gran about the apartment. She'll be so happy." She pushed the door open to her grandmother's room and stepped inside. "Gran! Just wait until you hear the—"

Her voice caught mid-word and Colt spun around as he shut the door. A woman stood beside Dorris's bed, smiling at Dani. She had brown hair cut like a boy's and wore a trim little dress with a checkered pattern. She looked like she'd been out for a casual date, not roaming the streets of a town on the edge.

Dani stepped closer, her eyes almost bulging. "Mom? Is that you?"

The woman beamed. "Hi Danielle. It's so good to see you."

CHAPTER SEVENTEEN

COLT

SUNNYVALE CONVALESCENT HOSPITAL
Eugene, Oregon
7:30 p.m.

HER MOM? COLT STARED AT THE WOMAN WHO LOOKED like Betty Crocker with her prim little outfit and sensible shoes. This was the woman who tried to sell Dani to a drug dealer? This was the woman sent to prison for armed robbery, too strung out to do anything but steal?

Colt turned to Dani. She looked as shocked as he felt. He closed the distance between them and stopped beside her. With a smile, he stuck out his hand. "Hi. I don't believe we've met. I'm Colt Potter."

The woman glanced down at his hand and the smile plastered across her face slipped a fraction. "Becky Weber."

Dorris snorted from the bed and Colt caught her eye

as he let Becky's hand go. From the way she held herself a bit to the side of the bed, and as far away from Dani's mom as she could, he could tell she wasn't buying it. Colt wasn't sure if he should, either. What were the chances a drug addict who let her daughter go hungry could clean up this fast?

Dani shifted her weight back and forth beside Colt. The charming and outgoing girl he'd had dinner with only an hour before was gone. Now she stared at the floor, fingers fidgeting with the cuff of her sweatshirt. He couldn't stand to see her like that all because of the woman standing a few feet away.

"Dani told me you disappeared before the power went out."

He could feel Dani's stare on him, but he didn't look her way. He needed to get a read on her mom. Friend or foe? Which was it?

Becky cocked her head to the side. "I'm sorry, how do you know my daughter?"

"He's my friend." Dani's words came out surly and thick. She still didn't look her mother in the eye.

"A much older friend."

Colt smiled. "I helped her out of a jam the other day and when I found out she was alone, I sort of took her under my wing. I have a hard time seeing kids go hungry."

Becky's eyes might have matched her daughter's in color, but the fire spitting from them told a whole different story. She glanced at her daughter. "I know I've been gone, but I've been thinking about you every singe day, sweetheart."

Dorris cleared her throat from the bed and Becky twisted around to glare. This woman wasn't who she claimed to be. Sure, she might be Dani's mother, but the Susie Homemaker act? Colt didn't buy it for a second.

He reached out and gave Dani's arm a squeeze. The girl had retreated into a shell of herself, barely able to look up or speak. Becky had really done a number on her. Colt resisted the urge to deck the woman and be done with the whole thing.

Becky spoke up again. "I hope you're ready for a new adventure, Dani. I've got some exciting news."

Dani's head jerked up and she stared at her mother without speaking.

"I've got us a new apartment that's three times as big as the old one. You get to have your own room and Dorris even gets to come live with us. Isn't that great?"

Dani glanced up at Colt, her eyes broadcasting fear and confusion.

He couldn't let her get hurt, not again. "Where is this place?"

Becky smiled. "The college. The National Guard have been *so* helpful. They've arranged everything."

Dani reached out and clutched Colt's arm. Her fingers trembled.

"What about Dorris's care? She needs a nurse."

Becky glanced back at Dorris. "We've gotten that covered. The staff here are thrilled to discharge her." Becky leaned closer and Colt caught a whiff of something floral. Was she wearing perfume? "You know it's not like they're at full staff these days."

Colt shifted to catch Dorris's eye. Did the old woman

want to leave? She sat on the bed, her face an unreadable mask. "Don't you think you should talk to her doctor?"

"Already did. All the paperwork's been taken care of and any minute now we should be getting the go-ahead to leave."

Oh. Colt blinked. He didn't know what the hell to do. Family drama wasn't his thing. If Dani's mother was on the up-and-up, then she should be the one to care for Dorris and Dani. But after everything the pair of them said about her, how could he believe anything she said?

If she really had been with the National Guard all this time, wouldn't he have run into her? He squinted in the dim light of the fading sun outside. Had he run into her and just not noticed?

The two weeks he'd spent on the college campus weren't the most aware of his life. Most of his hours revolved around Heather and the double bed they shared. For all Colt knew the woman standing across from him could have been sitting next to him at every meal and he never gave her a second glance.

Just as he was about to open his mouth, the door to the room opened and an orderly pushed a wheelchair through. Dani shrunk back, afraid of the orderly spotting her, but the man paid her no heed.

He smiled and stopped the wheelchair beside the bed. "All right, Mrs. Weber, we've processed your paperwork and you are all ready to go."

Dorris straightened up. "Are you sure everything's in order?"

"Oh, yes. The staff at the college hospital will take

over your care and see to it that you take your medicine."

Colt stood like a tall weed in a freshly mowed field, obvious and out of place. How could he protect Dani if she went to live with her mother? How could he not let her go?

He leaned down and whispered, "If you don't want to go with her, just let me know."

Dani didn't say anything, but Becky did. "I'm afraid that's not possible. Danielle is coming with me. She's my daughter. I'm her legal guardian."

Colt straightened back up. "She's fifteen. If she doesn't want to go with you, I'd say that under the circumstances, she shouldn't."

"And where is she going to go, exactly?"

He rolled his eyes. "You didn't seem to care much about that two weeks ago."

Dani grabbed his arm. "It's okay. I want to go with her."

Colt started. "You do?"

She nodded. "Yeah." A forced smile tipped up the corners of her lips. "You look great, Mom."

"Thanks, honey. Now help me get your grandmother into this wheelchair, will you?"

Colt couldn't believe Dani wanted to go with the mother who abandoned her time and time again and never once gave a damn whether she lived or died. He watched helplessly while they loaded Dorris into the wheelchair. Her wrinkled feet curled as they hung in the air, her legs too short to touch the ground.

Crouching in front of her, he smiled. "Are you sure you want to go, Dorris?"

She reached out and patted his hand. "If Dani is going, then I'll go, too."

"You don't have to."

Dorris glanced over at the orderly standing by the door. He hadn't even helped her into the chair. "Yes, I'm afraid I do. But don't worry, Dani won't be alone. I'll be there."

She meant well, but an old woman dying of cancer wouldn't be much help to Dani other than company. Colt couldn't help but feel this was all a scam, but he didn't know why or what it could be about. All he did know was that he was losing the one person who came to mean something to him in this world.

He reached out and took Dani's hand, crouching so she could look him in eye. "I know I said I was leaving, but I've changed my mind. I'm going to stay. So if you want to stay, it's okay. Just say the word."

She swallowed, eyes trained on his. They were full of sadness and something else he couldn't place. "I'll be okay, Colt. You can go."

Didn't she understand? She might be fine, but he wouldn't be. He squeezed her little hand. "I'm staying, Dani. If you need me, I'll be there. You just have to let me know."

All of a sudden she slipped her arms around his neck and buried her face in his shirt.

Her mother cleared her throat. "This is touching and all, but Dani, we really need to go. One of the soldiers is outside waiting with a truck. We need to get

Dorris loaded up and back to the campus before he goes out on patrol."

Dani pulled back, her eyes wet and shining. "Bye, Colt. Thanks for everything."

"Bye, Dani."

She pulled away and he stood up, watching as Becky wheeled Dorris toward the door.

"You need anything, you find me, Dani. Promise?"

Dani turned to look at him one last time. "I promise."

Colt watched the three women walk out of the door, and part of his heart went with them.

Nausea settled in the pit of his stomach. Dani's mother couldn't clean up that fast. Meth would take days to leave her system and then she'd be in massive withdrawal with no energy to do anything but sleep. Cravings should kick in and the woman would have done anything to stop them.

He spun around and rushed to the windows, peering down into the darkness at the camo-painted truck waiting outside. Becky didn't look like a meth-head. Her skin appeared healthy, her hair vibrant and clean, and she didn't have a single sore.

Colt paused. When she smiled, she didn't show her teeth.

The door to the truck opened and a man in a soldier's uniform stepped out. He helped load Dorris into the back and Dani followed. As he shut the door, he turned to Becky. They leaned together, but Colt couldn't see. Were they kissing or talking? He didn't know.

Becky rushed around to the passenger side and

hopped in and all of the hope and joy Colt experienced the last two days drove off in a humvee.

This wouldn't be the end of it. Colt wouldn't let this night ruin his newfound relationship with Dani. He promised to protect her and he would.

DAY EIGHTEEN

CHAPTER EIGHTEEN

COLT

Big Sky Sporting Goods
  Eugene, Oregon
  8:00 a.m.

The sporting goods store sat on the edge of Eugene, over a mile from the campus where Dani presumably now lived. Colt hated to leave her, but he needed supplies. He couldn't sneak into a fortified facility in jeans and dress shoes, even with all his skills.

He crouched in a rear stairwell to a building sharing the same loading zone, watching for activity. The place appeared empty. From the outside, it looked undisturbed, but that meant nothing. The army could have come in and ransacked the place or the owners could have cleared out the second the grid failed.

Colt stepped down off his perch and strode to the back door. His patience had been spent. Colt hoisted the

M-4 and took a deep breath. He lifted it up above his shoulder and with a brutal slice, he slammed it on the bottom corner of the door.

The glass warbled. *Shit.* He hated to waste ammo. Pulling out his Sig, he stepped back and aimed at the same spot. One shot and the door shattered, the tempered pieces falling like little pebbles. Colt raised the gun and stepped inside.

The smell hit him first.

Cloying and heavy, the stench of ripe death caught him off guard. He gagged.

No throwing up.

Swallowing down a wave of bile, Colt advanced into the store.

Apart from the putrid odor, nothing appeared disturbed. Racks full of everything from energy bars to lanterns to every kind of climbing rope still sat full and welcoming. Cases of freeze-dried camping food and the fuel to reheat them greeted him at the end of the aisle.

But that smell could only come from one thing: a body. It didn't make sense.

Colt walked down the aisle, rolling his feet with every step to keep his sound to a minimum. His pistol led the way, straight out in front of him, ready to fire. Every three steps, he swept the area, panning from left to right and back again.

With so much stock and so many places to hide, he would never be able to clear the store. Finding the source of the stench would have to do. He inhaled. It was stronger in the back.

After looping around the main aisle, Colt re-approached the rear of the store. A customer service bay for returns and questions sat behind the sales floor and Colt crept toward it. The smell intensified.

With his back close to the wall, Colt eased inside the space, skirting the counter as he squinted into the dark. No windows adorned the back area and the light from the main floor barely reached inside. He would need to use a flashlight.

Colt pulled out a little LED number he'd pocketed at the office supply store and held it in his left hand, bracing his pistol still gripped in his right. He clicked the little light on and swept the area. *Empty.*

Advancing toward the counter, he stayed close to the wall. Ten steps and he cleared the counter. Five more and he froze.

Three bodies sagged against the interior wall of the counter, leaning against each other like a decomposing family portrait. A father, a mother, and a child who couldn't have been older than Dani.

All shot in the head and dead at least a week.

Colt swallowed. What would make them choose this path? He glanced up. They were rotting inside a store that held everything they needed. Boots, tents, camp stoves, and food. Three people could survive for a year on just the supplies filling the store. Why would they do this?

He stepped closer and crouched to examine their bodies. The skin around the bullet holes sagged from decay, but Colt could still make out the stippling around the entry wounds. Close range. Personal.

Colt turned his attention to the floor around them. He frowned and peered around their folded hands.

No gun.

Either someone else took advantage of the situation and pilfered the necessary weapon, or these people didn't take the easy way out. They were murdered.

Colt stood up, hand pinching the back of his neck on reflex. Who would kill a family of shopkeepers but not raid the store?

He dropped his hand. Someone who would be back. If they hadn't had time to clear the place out or they needed more equipment to do the job right, then taking out the family first might be the easiest way. Leaving the bodies to stink up the place would keep interlopers out.

No one but a man used to gutting it out like Colt would even step inside. The locals? Not unless some militia lurked in the town, keeping a low profile. The motorcycle club was a contender.

Colt backed up, handgun ready, before stepping around the counter and onto the sales floor. What did the store have that would be so important?

Camping gear. Backpacks. Fuel and portable stoves. Everything a group would need to survive in the wilderness or a town without power.

Not just anyone could have killed those people. A wife and husband and their daughter? No way. It took callous planning and a disregard for human life. It was one thing to neutralize a threat. That's what Colt had done with the men in the street. He'd saved Dani from a fate he refused to imagine.

Colt paused. *Dani*.

If a secret force was building in the town, she would be in danger. He still didn't know what to make of her mother showing up looking every bit the model parent or the military carting them all off to the college campus. None of it made sense.

He felt like he had all the pieces of a puzzle staring him in the face, but he couldn't make sense of it because they were all upside down. But he knew Dani needed protection, maybe now more than ever.

Protection was something Colt could do no matter what. He strode into the store and headed straight for the boots. If he was going to scout out the National Guard and find out Dani's situation, he needed gear and supplies.

He slipped his dress shoes and nasty socks off his feet and wiggled his toes. Foot health was one of the most overlooked things in the field, but it could mean the difference between life and death. If blisters popped or skin rubbed raw, infection could set in.

So far, he'd avoided the worst of it, but his feet would thank him for the breathable wool socks he slipped on and the sturdy boots.

After dealing with his feet, Colt headed to backpacks, picking out two packs: a large bug-out one he could fill with all the gear he needed to live on his own, and a tight day pack for critical items that wouldn't weigh him down in a fight.

As he picked them up to walk away, Colt paused. Dani should have one, too. If there was even a chance she would need it, he should make it now, not later. Grabbing a smaller women's pack, he headed to the next department, ever vigilant for any noise inside the store.

So far, he'd been lucky. The light from the windows gave him enough visibility and he could ease through the store without alerting anyone outside. For all intents and purposes the place still looked locked and empty. It was only the back door that showed signs of Colt's presence, and not many people had a reason to enter the loading area.

Colt walked through the store on a mission, assembling everything in systematic, orderly fashion. Although taking his time meant he wouldn't be ready to hit the college-turned-military base until late, it was necessary. He needed to be ready.

Two hours later, he had three bags packed with a litany of items: sleeping bags, inflatable sleeping pads, a camp stove and fuel, freeze dried food, water filtration, first aid, bandanas and hats and extra socks and clothes, and a million other little things. He'd even changed into tactical gear, ditching the jeans for black cargo pants and the cotton T-shirt for a wicking fabric.

With a little preparation, he would be ready for a reconnaissance mission and possible extraction. All he had to do was find Dani first.

After hoisting his main pack onto his back, Colt added Dani's to his front and slung the little pack over his left arm. He had to be carrying a hundred pounds. Ultra-lighting, he wasn't, but it didn't matter. He could make it to Dani's apartment, recuperate, and make a plan.

Colt lumbered toward the back door, adjusting the

straps of the packs as he walked. At the broken door he hoisted himself through the opening, crab-walking through the remnants of the glass.

As he eased into the midday sun, movement caught his eye. A blur more than anything, at the edge of the building. He dropped the day bag, eased Dani's off his chest, and crouched behind it. The M-4 was strapped to his pack, lashed down with bungee cords. He would get it if he could.

First, he pulled his handgun out of its holster and felt to ensure the hunting knife he'd picked up in the store sat secure against his ankle. He waited for two minutes, scanning his field of view for movement. *Nothing.*

Maybe it had been a stray dog or a cat on the prowl, but Colt didn't think so. His hair on the back of his neck stood on end and his heart thudded like it did just before a conflict. Someone was out there. Waiting.

As he saw it, there were two options: retreat back into the store and wait the threat out, or go on the offensive. He'd already taken hours inside the store preparing. Dani could be on a truck halfway to Seattle by now. Or she could be hurt. Afraid.

Colt unclipped the waist strap of his pack and slid it to the ground behind him. He pulled the M-4 free and slung it over his shoulder where he could grab it in an instant. Colt wasn't a hiding sort of man. If someone out there wanted a fight, that's exactly what they would get.

CHAPTER NINETEEN

COLT

Big Sky Sporting Goods
  Eugene, Oregon
  11:00 a.m.

Colt side-stepped down the three stairs, his back scraping against the stuccoed wall as he went. Although he couldn't see anyone, standing against the beige wall of a building dressed in all black made him jumpy as hell. He needed cover and he needed it now.

Too bad there wasn't a tree or bush line easily accessible. Urban warfare was the worst. Colt crept to the corner of the building, constantly scanning his sightline for any movement. As he paused, shoulder an inch from the edge, a sound made him freeze.

Footsteps.

They were soft, intended to be silent, but Colt still picked them up. If it had been later, he could have used the sun to his advantage, scoping out shadows on the ground. But it seemed nothing was on his side except skill.

He took a few calming breaths and bent to the ground. The first two broken chunks of asphalt he found were too small, but the third had just the right heft and weight. With a strong hook, Colt tossed the rock well clear of the building.

The footsteps stopped, shuffled. *Voices.* They were in the alley to the side of the building. Colt thought about what he'd seen. Two dumpsters. A side door. Thirty feet to the main street.

He needed more of a diversion. He rushed back to the landing and unzipped the main compartment of Dani's pack. The store didn't carry handguns, but it did sell flares, so he'd stocked her pack. Colt pulled out the bright red flare gun and loaded it.

Sure, he could race back inside, try to fortify the door or find the stairwell that led to the roof and attempt to cherry pick off the assailants, but the likelihood of success was low. By then, they would be expecting him or already be inside the store.

The only thing Colt had going for him was surprise and the balls to take a risk. He cocked the flare gun and held it in his left hand while he positioned the M-4 in his right.

A deep breath later, he was good to go.

Easing the flare gun around the corner, Colt fired. The flare whooshed out of the chamber and Colt followed right behind. As he came out into the open the flare lit up the street, blazing bright red as it sailed straight for two men in army fatigues.

They shouted and ducked, jumping out of the way of the flare as it headed straight for them. Colt had a chance to take them out, but he hesitated. The army was after him? He began to lower the M-4 when one of them spotted him and opened fire. The shots went wide, hitting the pavement a few feet to Colt's left.

"Hey, I'm a friendly! Don't shoot!" Colt began to raise the M-4 above his head when the one on the right dropped to one knee. He was going to shoot Colt while he held the rifle in the air.

Shit. They obviously weren't interested in a friendly chat. Was this about the man he'd disarmed earlier or the one he'd saved Dani from? He didn't know and in that moment, couldn't care. No one was taking him out.

Colt dropped to the ground and rolled as a three-round burst landed in the spot he'd just been. He spun around to his chest and took aim. Three rounds, straight shot, right into the firing man's chest. One thing air marshals excelled at was hitting their targets. The soldier who'd shot at Colt didn't stand a chance. He crumpled to the ground.

Colt swung the rifle in the direction of the other man. He'd ducked out of the way, hiding behind a dumpster while Colt fired, but he hadn't done a good enough job. Colt fell to the ground, sighted his target and fired. The bullets pierced the soldier's leg exposed in the strip of space between the dumpster bottom and the ground.

Two down, more to go.

With a deep breath, Colt ran for the nearest dumpster. It was reckless, but so was lying on the ground with no cover. He couldn't retreat. Not now.

The metal side of the dumpster singed his skin as Colt slammed into it. The sun beat down on him from above, and although it was only March, Colt's shirt dripped in sweat.

The contents of the dumpster reeked, the smell overpowering his senses as he sucked in much-needed air. One soldier lay where he fell, bleeding out onto the asphalt. The other moaned and groaned from behind the second dumpster. Colt hadn't killed him. How many more were there?

He scanned the tops of the buildings. *Empty*. The rest of the alley, too. As he wiped at the sweat dripping into his eyes, an engine's rumble caught his ear.

The wounded soldier called out. "Over here, man!"

Colt could only handle so many at once. He eased back against the wall of the building, wedging tight between the brick and the dumpster. He caught sight of a pickup truck coasting up to the alley. It stopped on the street, side windows of the cabin just in view. Colt could make out the driver, but the rear doors were too tinted to see. The most it could hold was five, maybe six.

He could handle six.

Putting all his strength in to the effort, Colt shoved the dumpster. It rocked on its wheels but didn't move. He shoved again and it rolled an inch. It was enough.

He stuck the barrel of the M-4 through the gap and took aim at the window. *Plink, plink, plink*. The first shot sent a hole through the rear window, the second broke it, and the third landed square in the chest of the passenger. He didn't stand a chance.

The truck accelerated in an instant, charging into the alley like a bull in a china shop. It careened to a stop beside the wounded man. Colt took aim again. Firing into the windshield, he didn't stop until the entire thing shattered.

When he stopped firing, everything fell silent. Had he done it? Were they dead?

A volley of shots peppered the dumpster in response and Colt wedged tighter against the brick wall. He hid his feet behind the wheels, but it wasn't perfect. A good shot and he'd go down.

He needed to stop them. For all he knew guys were running away that very second, trying to get back to the unit. If they made it, a full-on manhunt would ensure. He'd be worse off than Harrison Ford in *The Fugitive*.

If he didn't neutralize the threat, he would never fulfill his promise to keep Dani safe. The more he thought about that girl, the more he couldn't leave her.

He pulled the flare gun out of a pocket on his pants and loaded another flare. They didn't have the best accuracy, but he had to try. With a steady grip, he fired at the now-gaping windshield. The flare arced in the air, cruising toward the truck in slow-motion.

As someone shouted, the flare cruised through the opening and landed inside the vehicle. Within a minute, a fire bloomed inside the truck, flames spreading higher and higher across the fabric seats. More shouts erupted.

In the chaos, Colt had his chance. He rushed forward, slinging the M-4 behind him in favor of his Sig.

While someone inside the truck batted at the flames, Colt advanced.

Twenty feet, then fifteen, then ten. He raced around the side of the dumpster to the wounded man. He lay on the ground, legs sprawled out in front of him, eyes vacant. In the scuffle, he'd bled out. Colt turned toward the truck, ducking to keep below the front grille.

Chaos raged inside, flames licking the roof. The door on the other side flew open and a hacking, coughing soldier tumbled out. The only one left.

Colt closed the distance in seconds and kicked the man in the ribs. He fell to his knees and Colt kicked him again.

Clutching his stomach, the soldier rolled over. Colt pointed the Sig right in his face. "Tell me why."

Coughing, the soldier shook his head.

Colt leaned closer. "Tell me why or I shoot you in the head."

The soldier doubled over, retching onto the ground. Colt took aim, but the man held up a hand and tried to speak.

"W-we—" He erupted into another fit of hacking and Colt leaned closer.

He never saw the knife coming.

The blade sliced through his pants and straight into his quadriceps, driving deep into the muscle. Colt reacted on instinct and the soldier collapsed on the ground, a single bullet in his head.

Damn it.

As the soldier's hand slipped off the knife hilt, Colt

staggered back. He surveyed the scene, pain blurring his vision.

Bodies everywhere.

Truck burning.

The smell of melting plastic and warping metal assaulted his nostrils and Colt spun around. He limped to the body of the soldier beside the dumpster. He leaned over the man and pulled up his shirt. Grunting against the pain, Colt unbuckled the rigger's belt and tugged it loose from the dead man's utility pants. The body flopped as he tugged, arms flailing about like a puppet on strings.

Sweat dripped off Colt's nose and his vision dimmed. He needed a damn tourniquet. At last, the belt gave way and he stumbled to the dumpster. Wrapping the belt around his thigh, a few inches above the knife that still stuck out of his leg, Colt cinched it so tight he cried out.

Only then did he remove the knife.

He leaned against the dumpster, fighting to stay conscious. As the moment of vertigo passed, he hobbled over to the other man on the ground and ripped off his belt as well. After making it back to the packs, Colt ripped into his and dug out the first aid kit and a bandana.

With his teeth locked together, he tore his pants wide enough to inspect the wound. A two-inch-long gash. Deep and still bleeding. He poured antiseptic on it and followed with gauze and the bandana. Only then did he apply the second belt, cinching it directly over the wound. It wouldn't seal it shut, but the double tourniquet would keep him from bleeding out before he got it closed.

As he zipped up his backpack, a huge boom erupted from the alley. A fireball rose in the air, followed by billowing smoke. The truck had exploded.

It was time to go. Colt eased his backpack onto his shoulders and grabbed the day pack as well. Dani's would have to stay behind. Putting as little pressure as feasible on his wounded leg, Colt stopped at each soldier, relieving the dead bodies of their weapons, radios, and ammo. He tossed all but one radio inside the burning truck and walked away.

A single man stood outside what used to be a bookstore, staring at him. From the pallor of his cheeks and the way his clothes hung his frame, the man looked like he hadn't eaten in days. He didn't say a word.

Colt gave him a nod and kept walking, the limp barely noticeable in comparison to the backpacks and rifles strung over his body. He looked like a ridiculous actor in an action hero movie, alive to fight another day. It wasn't that far from the truth.

He'd get somewhere safe, patch up his leg, and set off. The military wanted to find him? He'd make it easy. Colt would just go to them.

CHAPTER TWENTY

DANI

University of Oregon Campus
   Eugene, Oregon
   1:00 p.m.

Dani shoved the beef stew around the little tray. She'd already eaten the bread, jam, and chalky stuff the package claimed was peanut butter. Now the main dish sat in front of her congealing while she watched.

She should be thankful. The military picked her up and gave her a place to sleep and food to eat and never once asked if she'd broken some soldier's kneecap or watched Colt shoot three thugs who wanted to have a little fun.

Leaving Colt had been the right decision. He wanted to hit the road, she'd known that from the first moment they met. The words couldn't have been more plain: *I'm not a family man. I don't want to be a surrogate dad.*

No matter how many times she caught him smiling at her or seeming proud, Colt didn't want her in his life. Everything he did was to set her up to survive on her own: the supplies, apartment, self-defense skills. He didn't plan on sticking around.

Her mom showing up only sped up the process.

Dani glanced up at the entrance to the cafeteria. After dropping Dani off in her own room last night, her mother disappeared with Gran down the hall and Dani hadn't seen her since. She didn't know where Gran was and she couldn't risk going to find her.

What if that soldier she hurt was in the hospital? What if he recognized her and sent her to whatever worked as jail in this place? Juvie might have been a blessing in disguise when her mom fell off the wagon, but right now it could be a death sentence. Dani didn't trust anyone around here to keep their word. Not after that soldier tried to haul her away.

A woman sat down across from her and groaned as she looked at her plate. "Beef stew again? Who can eat this slop?" She rolled her eyes and picked up the package of bread. Her red curls bounced around her face as she tore the package open with her teeth.

Dani couldn't help but stare. She was beautiful.

"Got a problem, kid?"

Dani ducked her head. "No."

At last, the redhead got the package open and she let out a little whoop. After chomping down on the bread, she eased back in her chair. "Sorry I snapped at you. I get a bit hangry in the afternoon."

"It's okay."

The woman held out her hand. "I'm Heather."

Dani wiped her hand on her napkin and gave Heather's a quick shake. "Dani."

"Nice to meet you, Dani. Are you in college here?"

Dani shook her head. "Not old enough. I'm just a local."

Heather cocked her head. "Really? I didn't think they were letting any locals in here." She tore open the package of jam and slathered the contents on the rest of her bread. "You some politician's kid or something?"

"Nope." Dani pushed her beef stew around again. "What are they doing here?"

Heather shook her head. "Beats me. All I know is they asked all the college kids who had families they could reach to leave first thing. We showed up after our plane emergency-landed just outside of town. So far, they've let us stay, but I don't know any more than that."

Dani forked a bite of beef and popped it in her mouth. Colt said he arrived on a plane, too. Were they on the same flight? "An emergency landing sounds scary."

Heather leaned in, her eyes bright and full of excitement. "It was. I've been a flight attendant for five years, but I've never done anything like that. Our pilot, Captain Sloane? He was amazing. Everyone clapped when we landed."

Dani wished she could ask outright about Colt, but she didn't want to get him in trouble. "How did you all make it to Eugene? There's not a whole lot outside of town. You must have been in the mountains."

Heather nodded. "We were. But we had an air marshal on our flight and he walked into town, tracked down the National Guard, and they sent up some buses for us. We were here within twenty-four hours after the power grid failed."

An air marshal. That had to be Colt. Dani wanted to learn everything about him. What he did, where he'd been. There was so little she knew. In some ways it was pointless, the but the more she knew, maybe the easier it would be to hold onto his memory. "What's an air marshal?"

Heather snorted. "A big, fat jerk, that's what."

Dani raised her eyebrows.

"You really want to know?"

Dani nodded.

Heather forked a bite of carrot and pointed it at Dani as she spoke. "They're arrogant, conceited, selfish bastards. But they're really good in bed." She put the carrot in her mouth and chewed while Dani stared like she'd just seen her grandmother dancing.

"Oh, sorry, kid. You probably didn't need to know that last part."

"It's okay." Dani tried to play it off. "I don't mind. He was a real jerk, huh?"

"The worst." Heather shook her head. "Came onto me on the plane and sweet-talked me nonstop when we got back here. Two weeks go by, I think he's really into me, you know, and then, bam! He gets up one day and says he's leaving. That he's not a 'relationship man.' Whatever that means."

Heather flipped her hair behind her shoulder and stabbed another bite of food. "I swear if I ever see Colt Potter again, I'll have him arrested for fraud."

Dani swallowed. "I don't think you can do that."

"Then I'll lie! The jerk deserves it."

She couldn't believe it. Colt had been in a relationship with a woman as beautiful as Heather and he just got up one day and walked away? It didn't make any sense. When he said he didn't do relationships, he really meant it. Heather probably hadn't been rejected very often.

She seemed like a difficult woman to handle. Dani tried to smile. "What are you going to do now?"

"Wait until they finally let me go home, I guess. I've got a sister in Sacramento. I need to get back there. But every time I bring it up, I just get the brush off. It's like all these macho guys around here are in the middle of some big thing but they won't tell any of us civilians what's going on."

Dani chewed on her lip. It's exactly what Colt had said earlier. The military was up to something, but he couldn't figure it out. "Do you think they're getting ready to leave?" If they did, what would happen to Gran?

"I have no idea, sweetheart, but if they do, one of those guys is taking me with them." Heather looked down at her tray and snorted in disgust. "I'm throwing this slop in the garbage and finding a vending machine. Want to come?"

Dani shook her head. "No thanks."

"Suit yourself. Nice meeting you, kid." Heather stood up and dumped her tray in the trash before heading out the double doors.

Dani leaned back in her chair and looked around. Apart from a couple three tables over, an older woman by herself, and a man who looked like a professor, she was alone. She thought about all the things Heather had told her. How Colt had walked out with no notice, how the military was keeping everyone in the dark and not letting any townies into the campus.

She had woken up that morning depressed over saying goodbye to Colt, but now she knew it was the right decision. The last thing she wanted was to wake up one day and have him be gone.

After shoveling a few more bites in her mouth, Dani stood up and threw her trash away. The army had figured out how to get power to critical equipment and they'd rigged up portable showers down the hall. Just the thought of water pouring over her head was incredible. She reached back and felt beneath her ponytail to the wound on her scalp.

It still hurt, but a shower would probably be okay. She walked down the hall to her room and pulled open the door. Everything was as she left it. A twin bed, nightstand, and a single window to let in the light. She hadn't brought any of her things and she wasn't planning on it.

Although she could tell her mom about the apartment and the supplies Colt helped her gather, she wanted to keep that part of her life to herself. The little she'd seen of her mother had been positive, but Dani still didn't know if she could trust her.

Was she really sober? Had the military helped her like she claimed? Or was she just putting on a good act? Dani didn't know, but she hoped it was the former. Maybe the EMP shocked her mother into cleaning up for good.

She kept the positive thoughts in her mind as she headed to the shower. Halfway there, she froze. Her mother stood at the end of the hall, chatting with a soldier on crutches. Dani couldn't tell from her vantage point, but the hair and the shape of his head reminded her of the man who caught her on the street. The one who wanted to drag her back here and throw her in jail.

It can't be. If her mother was talking to him, was this all a setup? Did her mother plan on selling her out? Dani took a step back and collided with a warm body.

She spun around in a panic. "I'm sorry, are you okay?"

The soldier nodded. "I'm fine. Sorry to have startled you."

"It's okay."

"Danielle! Danielle, wait right there!"

Her mother's voice echoed down the hall and Dani glanced behind her. The soldier on crutches was hopping her way. *Crap.* She spun back around. "I've got to go. Sorry again."

"Dani! Wait!" Her mother's voice grew frantic. "Sir! Sir, stop that girl, please!"

Dani lunged around the soldier, but he reached out and grabbed her arm.

"Let go of me."

"I'm afraid I can't do that."

Her mother jogged up, winded and out of breath. With her mouth sagging open for air, Dani could see all her rotting teeth. Even if her mom cleaned up on the outside, the drugs had taken a toll no shower and new clothes could repair.

She clenched her side as she spoke. "It's about time I found you. There's someone here you need to meet."

CHAPTER TWENTY-ONE

DANI

University of Oregon Campus
Eugene, Oregon
2:00 p.m.

Dani tugged on her arm, but the soldier to her right still held on, his grip tight enough to bruise. "Let me go!"

"Is she your daughter?"

Dani's mom nodded. "Yes, sir. I can take her from here. Thank you." She reached out and grabbed ahold of Dani's arm even harder than the soldier, her nails digging into Dani's skin through her sleeve.

"Mom! You're hurting me!" Dani practically shouted in her mother's face, hoping someone would intervene.

No one paid them any mind.

Her mother eased closer, voice barely above a harsh whisper. "It's not nice to run away from your mother when she's speaking to you."

Dani bit her cheek to keep from lashing out again. No one there would help her. She would need to wait for an opening and exploit it. Just like Colt had said.

The soldier on crutches hobbled down the hall. At ten feet away, Dani confirmed it was the same one who caught her in the store. The guy she kicked and who lost his rifle to Colt. Despite the smile on his face, he would never be her friend. He would never be on her side. She probably ended his career.

"I'm not going anywhere with that guy."

Her mother dug her nails in harder. They had to be drawing blood. "You don't have a choice."

Dani sucked in a breath as the soldier stopped in front of her. "Is there a problem?"

"No. Dani's just anxious to talk to you. Isn't that right, dear?"

She pretended her lips were sewn shut and scowled instead.

Her mother made an excuse. "Typical teenager. You know how crabby they can be without enough sleep."

The soldier eyed her up and down. "Take her down the hall. Follow the signs to the auditorium. Room 105."

Dani swallowed. That wasn't anywhere near her room. The hair on the back of her neck rose. What was her mother planning? Did she even know what this man wanted to do with her?

She focused on the woman who never did a nice

thing without a motive. A shower and some makeup and decent clothes covered up the ugliness, but it still lurked beneath the surface. From the way she gripped her arm, to the fake sweetness on her tongue as she talked to the soldier, Dani saw it all. Her mother hadn't changed.

When she'd first seen her the night before, she'd let herself hope. She'd foolishly gone along with her because deep down somewhere, Dani was still a little girl who wanted a mom who cared. A mom who loved her.

"How long will it take?" Her mother's words echoed in her head.

The soldier sneered. "Depends on how cooperative she wants to be. I'll meet you there." He turned on his crutches and hopped back the way he'd come, his blocky head bobbing up and down with every sweep of his injured leg.

"Come on, you heard him. Let's go." Her mother tried to pull her along, but Dani resisted.

She leaned back, balancing on her heels as her mother yanked her arm. "What's in room 105?"

"It's nothing. Just move."

"No."

Her mother puffed out a breath. "Can't you for once not be a spoiled little brat? I need you to do this for me."

Spoiled? Her mother had the nerve to call her spoiled? She tugged her arm again and pulled her mother off balance.

Her mother cursed and glanced around the hall. Whatever she saw seemed to satisfy her and she used all her feeble strength to drag Dani a handful of steps. She couldn't let her mother take her to room 105 and whatever that soldier had planned.

As her mother took another step, Dani reared back, tugging against her mother with all her might. Her mother stumbled and her grip on Dani's arm loosened. The second her mother released her, Dani spun away. Her footsteps pounded on the linoleum floor, echoing against the walls.

"Danielle!"

No stopping. No looking back. She would get away from that woman and whatever horrible plan she'd concocted. No one was going to trap her in some room she couldn't escape.

Dani neared the end of the hall and slowed to round the corner.

She didn't see the rifle until too late. The stock slammed into her shoulder and Dani flew back, arms and legs circling in the air like a cartoon character. She hit the ground hard on her butt and kept going, falling back until her head slammed onto the floor.

All the air rushed from her lungs. She gasped like a beached fish.

Hands wrapped around her arms and hauled her upright while the room spun. Her vision dimmed, telescoping into a tunnel ringed in black. A humming eclipsed all sound in her ears and Dani fought the urge to vomit.

Cold metal slapped her wrists and Dani tried to speak. "Wh-What—"

"Shut up before I knock you out."

She didn't have to be told twice. Dani couldn't stay

conscious even if she wanted to. The ground loomed, her vision failed, and Dani passed out.

* * *

"DO IT AGAIN."

Cold water drenched Dani from above, soaking her hair and running in rivulets down her face. She blinked and tried to lift her hand to wipe it away. Her arm wouldn't budge.

"She's coming around."

"It's about damn time."

Dani opened her mouth and water droplets landed on her tongue. She smacked and tried to speak. "Wh-What's wrong?"

"Aw, how cute. She's talking." The voice turned cruel. "Smack her. That should wake her up."

A flat, hot palm landed hard on her cheek and Dani's head careened to the right. She blinked again and the world came into focus.

She sat in a chair in the middle of a room, a soaked blanket spread out beneath her. Zip ties secured her hands to the back of the chair and an empty bucket sat on the floor beside her feet.

"Where's the man who rescued you?"

Dani snapped her head up and the quick movement roiled her gut. She fought back the bile rising in her throat. An army soldier stood in front of her, older than the others she'd seen before. His uniform looked pressed and clean, and he'd shaved within the past day.

His blue eyes honed in on her face, and he asked his

question again. "Where's the man who took you from Sergeant McAllister?"

"Who's that?"

Her voice sounded thick and foreign.

"That would be me. The guy you stomped on, remember?"

Sergeant McAllister's face loomed too close, his big head eclipsing all but the overhead lights from her field of view.

She smacked her lips and tried to remember how to talk. "H-How's the leg?"

He snorted and backed up, throwing his arm out as he pointed. "You see? She's nothing but a punk. I told you we won't get anything out of her."

"Patience is a virtue, Sergeant."

The blue-eyed man never stopped staring at her. His gaze made Dani squirm. She looked away. "I don't know what you're talking about."

"Yes, you do." He took a step closer. "Colt Potter. Where is he?"

"How should I know?"

"You were with him last night."

Dani twisted around, looking for her mother. Had she told them about Colt? Did they want him for the assault on Sergeant McAllister? Did they know about the murders?

When she didn't see her, she sagged against the chair. No way would she rat him out. "The guy's gone. The second you all picked me up, he left. I think he said he's headed to California." Lies came easily. She'd learned from the best.

"No." The senior soldier shook his head. "He's still here."

She shrugged but her shoulders barely moved thanks to the restraints. "Sorry."

"You aren't yet, but you will be."

Dani's eyes narrowed. What was so important about Colt? "What do you want him for? It's not like he's an AWOL soldier or something."

"He's wanted for questioning."

"About what?"

"That's classified."

Dani rolled her eyes. If they weren't going to tell her what this whole interrogation was about, she wasn't going to give them any information. "I don't know where he's at."

"Can you get in touch with him?"

"I don't know how."

"Think." The man wasn't giving her an inch. Ordinarily, Dani faced these sorts of questions from nosy teachers or the occasional social worker. Enough teenage bravado and they gave up. It wasn't that she didn't want the help, but she knew what would happen: foster care. Bouncing around from home to home with people who didn't really want her, just the paycheck the state gave them.

No thanks. She'd rather be with her mom. At least she knew what she was going to get with her. Dani glanced around again, twisting until the zip ties pinched her wrists. "Where's my mom?"

"She's busy."

"Doing what? Snorting crystal?"

"Visiting your grandmother."

Dani's face fell. In the commotion of the morning, she'd forgotten about Gran. "Where is she? Can I see her?"

"I'm afraid your grandmother isn't well."

Dani pulled against the zip ties. "What do you mean?"

"She has advanced stage-four liver cancer."

The words hit Dani like a sucker punch. She leaned back against the seat.

The soldier smiled, his eyes twinkling like a bright summer day. "Didn't you know?"

"She was in remission."

He tilted his head and gave her a small, pitying smile. "It came back." The soldier lifted his hand and examined his fingernails like they held the secret to life. "The doctors here found tumors in not just her liver, but her lungs, too. Once it's gotten that bad..." He smiled as he lifted his head. "I'm afraid it's just a waiting game, really."

Dani swallowed. "I want to see her."

"Not until you tell us where to find Colt."

She shook her head. "No. You let me see my grandmother and then I'll tell you whatever you want to know."

He glanced at his watch. "I suppose a few minutes with her won't hurt. Assuming she's still breathing."

Dani blinked back the beginning of tears. Seeing Gran eclipsed everything else.

If she could just talk to her... Dani glanced back up

at the man in charge. He'd stepped away to speak to another soldier. If he was lying, she would never tell him anything.

But if he told the truth, Dani didn't know what she would do.

CHAPTER TWENTY-TWO

DANI

University of Oregon Hospital
Eugene, Oregon
3:30 p.m.

THE HALLS OF THE HOSPITAL WERE WAY TOO QUIET. Places like these were usually filled with whirring machines and constant beeping in a hundred different tones. Not now.

Apart from a few LED lanterns set up here and there, the whole hospital was dark and eerie. Dani walked along the corridor, an army guy beside her. The rifle didn't scare her, maybe it should have, but after seeing Colt disarm the other man, it didn't hold the same mystique.

She glanced at his profile. Short hair. Clean-shaven. She guessed about twenty-five, but she'd never been good at age. Everyone much older than her was just an adult until they hit the elderly stage. *Like Gran.*

She tried to get some information out of him. "Why's it so quiet? I thought you all had wind turbines running this place."

The soldier made some sort of noise in response. Was that a grunt?

"Is there something wrong with the power source? I thought it was better than coal? That's what they said in school."

He didn't even blink. After a few more failed attempts, Dani rolled her eyes and kept walking. They stopped outside a room with light filtering underneath the door.

"Is this it?"

He waved her forward and Dani swallowed. *I can do this.*

She pushed the door open and stepped into the room. A single lantern sat beside a hospital bed. The frail old woman lying against the pillows almost disappeared into the white sheets. Her skin had grown ashen, her lips pale and lifeless.

Was she already gone?

Dani rushed up to the bed and picked up her grandmother's hand. Warm, but barely.

Gran's eyelids flickered. When did she get so sick?

"Danielle. You're all right."

Dani pressed her lips together. Gran looked so weak and small. "Why didn't you tell me?"

Gran's lips worked into a half-smile. "Didn't want to worry you."

"I could have helped. Done something."

"You have a cure for cancer?"

Dani dropped her gaze. "I could have made you more comfortable."

Gran squeezed her hand. The gesture was feeble, but it meant so much. "I love you, Danielle. I'm sorry I haven't always been there for you."

"Gran, stop it. You're here now."

Her grandmother swallowed and closed her eyes. "Not for long."

"What?" Dani leaned closer. "Gran, no!" Clutching her grandmother's hands, Dani leaned closer.

Her grandmother fixed her eyes on Dani, fierce and bright beneath her wrinkled brow. "Be careful, Dani."

Dani blinked. "What?"

Her grandmother's voice dipped lower, turning almost guttural as she ground the words out. "Your mother can't be trusted. Neither can these men. Find Colt. You can trust him." She exhaled and a calmness came over her. "He's a good man, Danielle. Like my Ricky."

Dani opened her mouth to ask what Gran meant, but the old woman collapsed back onto the bed, her breathing labored and shallow. Spinning around, Dani found the soldier standing beside the door, more guard than anything.

"There's something wrong! Call a doctor."

The soldier didn't move.

"Didn't you hear me? She's sick. She can barely breathe. Call a doctor!"

He cast a lazy glance in her direction. "There's no doctor available."

"That's ridiculous. The army transferred her here so she would have better care. There has to be a doctor."

The soldier exhaled and finally looked her way. "No doctor can help her. The only people who get sent to this part of the hospital are ones who don't make it out. The higher-ups don't want to waste the power on them."

Dani's eyes widened as she stared at him. The whole thing had been a lie? They weren't going to help Gran get better? Dani spun back around to face the only woman who mattered in her life.

She looked so peaceful on the bed, eyes closed, lips curved in a slight smile. Dani leaned forward. "Gran? Gran are you all right?"

When her grandmother's eyes didn't flutter and her lips didn't move, Dani leaned closer, practically crawling on top of the bed to feel her grandmother's breath. There wasn't any.

No. No way. This isn't happening.

Dani grabbed her grandmother by the shoulders and shook, gently at first, then harder and harder until the old woman's head wobbled around like a bobblehead on a runaway car's dash.

"No, Gran. No! I need you." A cry tore from Dani's lips, rising up her throat like a freight train full of grief and sadness. Gran couldn't leave. She couldn't leave her all alone with no one but her mother.

She shook her again, messing up her grandmother's hair, tossing her lifeless hands about the bed. But it was no use. Gran was gone.

Dani choked out a sob and took hold of the roll bars on the bed to clamber over the side. She made room for herself next to Gran. Her body was still warm. Dani snuggled in so close.

Her tears ran over her cheeks and onto the sheets, soaking them as she held onto Gran's arm. Dani cried and cried until there weren't any tears left in her body. She didn't know why the soldier left her there, clutching at her grandmother like she could will her back to life, but Dani didn't care.

She wouldn't leave until someone dragged her away. Dani could pretend they were sleeping like they used to do on the couch in the living room after her mother had gone away. All those nights when Dani never slept because she couldn't trust the night.

The night was when the monsters came. When her mother's boyfriend showed up and pumped her full of drugs and chased Dani around the house.

Dani closed her eyes. She would take a little nap and they would both wake up. It was all just a nightmare.

Memories of being very small and curling up just like she did now filled her mind. Little snapshots of a time before she understood life....

The smaller she curled up, the harder she was to find.

Dani closed her eyes tight, squeezing until colors danced across the blackness. If she lay very still, the monsters couldn't find her.

Small and quiet like a little mouse. She could ignore the rumble in her belly, the thirst down the back of her throat, the things that crawled across her legs in the dark.

Hide, Dani, hide.

She twisted even tighter, knees bumping her chest, arms wrapped like wires around her shins. Don't cry. Don't even breathe.

"Dani!"

Her mother couldn't find her.

"Dani!"

She wouldn't find her. Not today.

"Dani!" Hands gripped her shoulders and hauled her up. Dani lashed out, screaming and punching. They wouldn't take her. They wouldn't.

"She's dead, Danielle!"

Dani blinked her swollen eyes open. She wasn't a little girl anymore, hiding in the back of her closet. She was fifteen and the only woman who ever loved her was gone.

A soldier dragged her off the bed and tossed her into a vacant chair. She pushed her matted hair off her face and watched in horror as the man unceremoniously kicked off the brake on Gran's bed and wheeled her lifeless body out the door.

Only then did she notice her mother. She sat in a chair across the room, looking every bit as phony as a three-dollar bill. The clothes and the shower and the self-righteousness didn't hide a thing.

Dani scrubbed at her tear-stained cheeks. "How could you do this?"

Her mother glanced at the empty doorway and

shrugged. "I needed you."

Dani started. "What did you say?"

"The soldiers wanted you."

That didn't make any sense. Dani didn't have anything they could want. She was just a kid. "Why would they want anything to do with me?"

Her mother leaned back in the chair and crossed one leg over the other. She flicked her foot up and down like the whole situation bored her. "At first it was just payback for breaking that guy's knee."

Dani swallowed. "And then?"

"Once they found out you were with that guy, what was his name... Cash, Cole...?"

"Colt."

Her mother snapped her fingers. "Yeah, that's it. I knew it was weird. Anyway, after they found out you were with him, they wanted you for a whole other reason."

This was all about Colt? Dani sucked in a breath to keep from screaming. "Gran was fine in the nursing home. If you hadn't brought her here... If you had just stayed the hell away from us... She would still be alive."

"*Pfft.*" Her mother waved at her like she was an annoying gnat buzzing around her head. "Did you see her, Dani? She's been dying for years. The cancer never really went away."

Dani froze, her fingers splayed on the arms of the chair, unable to move. That couldn't be true.

"Didn't she tell you?" Her mother shook her head. "That's so like Dorris to keep secrets. The fact she hung on this long has been a miracle. Think about it, Dani. If she'd been healthy, she'd have gone home. I wouldn't have been stuck with you all these years."

Stuck with me? Dani glanced out the window and tried to pull herself together. Her mother had said worse, done worse. This was nothing new. "Gran loved me."

"And now she's dead. You need to get over it and grow up."

Dani leaned back in the chair and crossed her arms. "Like you give a shit about me."

Her mother said nothing. The silence was damning.

After a few minutes, Dani pushed the stabbing pain in her heart down so far it only ached. "What do they want?"

"To know where that guy is hiding."

"And if I refuse to tell them?"

Her mother smirked. "I've heard they can be real persuasive."

Dani snorted in disbelief. "What's in it for you?"

"A clean record. A new place to live and new clothes. All the food and water I want. And this." She rolled up her sleeve to show off a clear, square patch.

"A nicotine patch?"

"Fentanyl." Her mother beamed like she'd won first prize in a baking contest. "All the fentanyl patches I could ever want."

Dani rocked back in the chair. *Drugs?* The army offered to dope her mother up just for the chance to get Colt? "Why do they want Colt so bad?"

Her mother lowered her sleeve. "How the hell should I know?"

Colt had walked out of the college campus a free man. Okay, so maybe he'd relieved a soldier of his weapon to do it, but no one chased him down then. They couldn't be so hot to get him because of a simple sleight of hand, could they?

Dani chewed on her nail as she thought about Gran. Dorris Weber loved her more than anything else in the whole world. Gran told her not to trust anyone around here. Not her mother, not the soldiers.

Only Colt.

Gran had always been right before, so she had to be right now. Dani needed to warn Colt, but they would never let her leave. As she thought over what to do, a commotion sounded in the hall. Her mother stood up. "Look alive, sweetheart. It's time to talk."

CHAPTER TWENTY-THREE

DANI

52 Houghton Street, Apartment 310
  Eugene, Oregon
  4:30 p.m.

With every stair, Dani made a point of stomping. Her sneakers slammed into the steps so hard, her feet ached, but she didn't care. The louder, the better. A bruised foot was nothing compared to whatever these guys had in mind for Colt.

The soldier ahead of her twisted around and glared, but she ignored him. If Colt was inside, she would give him fair warning they were coming. No way would she be a surprise attack.

When they reached the top floor, Dani pointed at the apartment door. "It's that one."

The soldier cast her a sharp glance. "You're not playing us, are you kid?"

"No." She kicked at the ground, pretending not to care. "What's the point?" If they thought she was a sullen, insolent teenager, maybe they would give up and let her go. She could play that part. All she had to do was act like her mother.

The soldier unlocked the door with the key Dani had found inside the apartment the day before and entered, gun up and ready. Two other soldiers brushed past Dani and followed the first inside.

After a handful of minutes, they gave the all clear and Dani walked in with the older soldier from before following behind. The other men kept calling him "colonel." From his pompous attitude, Dani assumed he was in charge.

A young soldier spoke up. "He's not here."

"Thanks for the obvious report, Sergeant." The colonel walked around the space, his hands clasped behind him as he took it all in. He addressed Dani. "How long were the two of you here?"

"Only a day."

"You both planned to stay here?"

Dani nodded. "Colt slept on the couch." She didn't know why she volunteered that last little bit, but she couldn't help it. Colt was a good man. They should know that.

"Where could he be, Danielle?"

"I don't know." She turned to the windows and looked out on Eugene, still as quiet as ever. "He's probably out gathering supplies. Or maybe he's gotten wind of you and he's already on the run."

"We know for a fact that isn't true."

Dani spun around, her anger finally bubbling to the surface. "This is ridiculous. First you lie to me and tell me my grandmother will get the best care with you, then you pump my mother full of drugs so she'll do whatever you want, now you want me to tell you where to find Colt? Are you crazy? The man hasn't done anything to you."

"On the contrary." The colonel stepped close enough for Dani to see the lines around his eyes. He had to be in his early fifties. "This morning, he killed four of my men, set their truck on fire, and disappeared."

Dani stumbled back. She'd watched Colt kill the motorcycle guys in the street, but he'd done it to protect her. "There had to be a good reason."

"No." The soldier shook his head. "No reason. He ambushed and killed them. It's that simple. One got away and reported the entire thing. He murdered my men for no reason."

Colt would never do something like that. If he killed those men, they deserved it. "I don't believe you."

The soldier shrugged. "Believe what you want, but you will help me find him."

"Colonel Jarvis, sir. I found these clothes in the bathroom hanging up to dry." The soldier held up some of Colt's things. "They must be his."

"Good work, Corporal." Jarvis glanced at Dani. "Is that true?"

Dani nodded. "Yes. Those are his."

"Good. Then we'll just have to wait him out. Men, set up a temporary base camp. Move whatever you have to move, do whatever you have to do, but I want this place up and running in the next hour. Understood?"

"Yes, sir!" All three men shouted out in unison and rushed off to do the colonel's bidding.

Dani kept her expression even, but on the inside she was freaking out. They couldn't stay in her apartment. With all the windows, they would spot Colt coming before he made it inside. They would be ready and waiting and he would never have a chance.

She had to do something. Chewing on her lip, Dani thought it over. What could she do? There had to be a way to warn him. Dani glanced around the apartment, eyes flitting over the desk, the couch, the rug, still rolled up and shoved out of the way.

Then she saw the empty bag of sunflower seeds. She turned around. "Colonel Jarvis?"

"Yes?"

She chose her words carefully. "Were you telling the truth about those men? Colt really did kill them for no reason?"

"Yes, child. That's the truth."

She nodded like she'd come to a decision. "Then I'll help you. I know how to get in touch with him."

The man inhaled, his chest swelling out in satisfaction. "Tell me."

"I just need some masking tape and a clean window."

Five minutes later, Dani stepped back from the window and exhaled. The masking-tape X took up all of the pane and Dani was sure it could be seen from a few blocks away.

"That's it? Tape in a window?"

She glanced back at the colonel. Had he never watched TV? "It's from a show we both like."

Colonel Jarvis snorted. "And it will work?"

Dani kept her smile to herself. "It's our signal. If he sees it in the window, he'll come. It's just a matter of time."

The colonel smiled at her. "Good work. I like it when my subordinates think on their feet." He glanced at the soldiers busy converting the kitchen table to a mobile work area. "After you boys are set up, make sure this girl gets some dinner, will you?"

"Yes, sir!"

Dani glanced back at the window. She hoped Colt would understand. His life depended on it.

* * *

AFTER A MEAL OF ANOTHER MRE AND A BOTTLE OF water, Dani curled up in the papasan chair in the corner of the living room. With her hood pulled up over her head and a blanket draped across her middle, she could keep watch over the soldiers as they worked.

At first, they spoke in low, hushed voices, glancing up every few sentences to check on her. She never moved. Half an hour into her routine, they stopped paying her any mind. Their voices grew louder and Dani listened.

"So far the platoon has cleared sections one through seven."

"How many casualties?" Colonel Jarvis stood beside the kitchen table, staring down at a large map. Dani couldn't see it from across the room, but the way they talked, it had to be Eugene.

"Thirty-four, sir, if you include our own."

Dani swallowed down her shock. Thirty-four people were dead? From what?

"Any riots? Pockets of organized resistance?"

"Not more than a few houses, sir. Over on Julep Street, a group of homeowners banded together and tried to hide in a cellar. The place had been stocked to the gills with canned goods and paper products."

"Where are the homeowners now?"

The soldier paused. "Dead, sir."

Dani shuddered and the colonel glanced her way. His voice dipped and she strained to hear the words. "Tell them to proceed with the remaining sectors. Once the neighborhoods have been disarmed, we can work on processing through the stores. The important thing is removing the weapons."

"Yes, sir."

Nothing the colonel said made sense. They were going door-to-door and disarming civilians? Why?

The colonel leaned over, his palms resting on the table. "How are we on converting the freshman dorms to housing?"

"Good, sir. The initial clear out is complete. Once we've added beds to a few rooms and shut down the bathrooms, we should be good to go."

"Excellent. Start bringing in the eligible residents as soon as possible. The faster we can contain them in our environment, the easier they will be to control."

"Sergeant Ferguson, talk to me about the fuel situation."

"It's going well, sir. We've drained all the cars within a two-mile radius and are expanding from there. We have enough supply to run the generators for about two months and all of our requisitioned vehicles."

"We need more. Tell the supply soldiers to double their efforts."

"Yes, sir."

Dani clenched her fists beneath the blanket to keep from shaking. These weren't orders from the state or the federal government. They couldn't be. Stealing from the residents in town? Shooting those who resisted? Rounding everyone up and putting them in dorms?

She thought about all the lies they told. They weren't relying on nearby wind turbines or helping keep the town safe. They were organizing a militia. A full-on military dictatorship with Colonel Jarvis in command. She had to warn Colt. They had to find a way to get out of there.

CHAPTER TWENTY-FOUR

COLT

Eugene Corner Pharmacy
Eugene, Oregon
5:30 p.m.

Knife wounds hurt like an SOB. Colt leaned back against the exterior wall of the pharmacy, breathing in and out until the wave of pain passed and he could walk again. He'd made it about a half a mile carrying two packs and a barrage of weapons until the pain in his leg made walking impossible.

He stumbled inside and set his gear down, opting to keep a single rifle and his handgun on his body. The pharmacy looked the same as when they left it not that long before. Nothing in the town of Eugene, Oregon made sense. Why were some shops smashed up, but others fine? Where were all the people?

Why the hell did the army try to kill him? What did he ever do to them?

He groaned and kept walking. The tourniquet he'd fashioned out of belts worked well, but he needed to disinfect the wound and sew it shut. He hobbled into the back, using the still-standing shelves as support for his leg as he went. After at least half an hour of fruitless searching, he finally found what he needed: a suture kit.

He eased down onto the floor and exhaled. This part would suck. If he didn't get the tourniquets off and the wound closed up, he'd be at risk for losing too much blood flow in his leg. Too long without adequate blood supply and his tissue would start to die. If that happened, he was done for. Not exactly a whole lot of surgeons around to cut off his leg or a working prosthetics department to make him a new one.

With a deep breath, Colt loosened the belt cinched across the wound. Hot searing pain flared from his thigh down, whooshing like hot lava through his muscles. He dropped the blood-soaked belt on the floor and eased the bandana and gauze away from the wound. As he pulled the skin apart, blood oozed thick and fresh from the cut.

He grimaced and grabbed the alcohol. The smell hit his nose as he opened it and Colt exhaled. The second the liquid hit the wound, he cried out, but he kept pouring, his hand shaking from the agony.

As the pain subsided, Colt took a look at the gash. It was deep, but straight into his quadriceps. It didn't appear to puncture a major artery or twist and wreak internal damage. Thank God the soldier could only reach his leg.

If he'd stabbed him in the gut, Colt would be dead.

After disinfecting his hands, he tore open the suture kit and pulled out the needle. It wouldn't be the first time he'd been stitched up without anesthetic, but it would be the first time he'd done it to himself.

With agonizing slowness, Colt stitched the wound closed, jabbing the needle in one side and out the other, pausing only when he teetered on the verge of passing out. It took way too long, but he didn't have a choice.

He stared at his leg. Expert tailor he was not. If it healed, he'd have a nasty scar. But he'd take the ugliest scar in the world if it meant he still had a serviceable leg.

After confirming the stitches would hold, Colt applied a fresh bandage and released the other belt still clamped around his upper thigh. The fresh injection of blood down his leg didn't hurt this time and he leaned back against the wall in relief.

He'd been in situations like this before.

On his own. Wounded. Still on a mission.

But never in the United States and never against the supposed good guys.

All he could think about was Dani and where she was and what the army wanted with her. No matter how much she claimed to want to go with them, it didn't sit right with Colt. After the ambush, he knew there was more to it.

Once he felt good enough to stand, he made his way over to his pack, testing his leg. *So far, so good.* The stitches seemed to do their job. He changed out of his pants, opting for a new, non-blood-soaked pair, and popped an antibiotic pill from the stash he'd acquired in his earlier visit.

The whole afternoon, he'd been thinking. The town was too quiet. Even with the National Guard on patrol, people would be out milling about. Neighbors would be talking with neighbors. Shopkeepers would be trying to run their businesses. Instead, everyone hid like they were afraid to be seen.

Those men he passed on the street with Dani ran the second they were spotted. People didn't act like that unless they were terrified. It could have been a reaction to the motorcycle gang; they sure seemed full of bravado. But Colt didn't think so. It had to be the army.

Colt hoisted his pack onto his back, trying his best to avoid too much pressure on his injured leg. After grabbing the rest of his gear, he eased out of the pharmacy and back onto the road.

Opting for a side street, he hobbled down the sidewalk, passing cute little cottages with white picket fences and trailing flowers running up the mailboxes. Halfway down the street, a curtain in a front window fluttered. Colt stopped in front of the house.

Fresh paint, a well-tended flower garden. A welcome sign on the porch. A place where a neighbor would come out and say hello. Not today.

Colt kept walking. As he neared the end of the street, a little happy dog tore up between a pair of houses and stopped on the sidewalk. Its brown and gray fur looked a bit dull, but the tiny thing made up for it with a huge voice.

"Hey there." Colt tried to talk to it. He'd never been good with dogs.

A woman rushed up, skirts billowing as she ran. "Lottie, come here! You can't be out. You know that!"

"I think she likes me."

The woman looked up from the sidewalk, her black hair falling over her face as she stared. She rose up without saying a word, but Colt held up his hand.

"Please, can I talk to you?"

She glanced around the street, eyes quick and fearful. "You shouldn't be out here. No one is supposed to be out here."

"I don't understand. What's going on?"

"Where have you been?" She looked him over, pausing on the two backpacks and his beard. "Out in the wilderness?"

"The college campus."

The woman's eyes went wide and she clutched the little dog to her chest as she stood up. "Are you one of them?"

"Who?"

"The militia."

"You mean the National Guard?"

She shook her head. "That's what they say, but it can't be true. Not after what they've done."

Colt glanced around. "I was with a plane that crash-landed north of here. I hiked down to town and got buses for all the passengers. The National Guard put them up at the college." He narrowed his eyes. "Are you saying the National Guard has done something?"

Her lips thinned. "They aren't the National Guard. They came through here last week, dragged all of us out of our homes. Confiscated all weapons, inventoried our food." She glanced down at the little dog. "Took everyone's pets."

Colt's eyes went wide. "They took animals?"

She nodded. "And they didn't bring them back."

Colt reeled. "Did they tell you all to stay inside?"

She nodded. "No one can be seen on the streets. If we're caught talking, we'll be taken away." She stepped closer. "No one who's ever taken away comes back."

He needed to let her go. "Thank you for taking the chance to talk to me." He held out his hand. "Colt Potter."

She shook it. "Melody Harper."

"If you ever need anything, Melody. I can help."

Melody's face pinched. "What can one man do?"

Colt smiled. *A hell of a lot.* "Take care." He turned to go, more confident in his ability to make it to the apartment.

The National Guard unit had gone rogue. Now everything made sense. The patrols, the curfew, the refusal to let anyone leave the college campus. They were in the process of completing a military takeover of the entire town. In a few weeks, the entire town of Eugene would be working for Colonel Jarvis whether they liked it or not.

Colt needed to get to Dani's apartment and regroup.

If he could rest up and elevate his leg, he could come up with a plan.

The trek was slow going. He didn't approach her street until the daylight dimmed and dusk set in. Maybe that's why the light in the apartment caught his eye from so far away.

Colt pressed his body against the wall of the nearest building, hoping to shield himself from view. He squinted into the gloom. *That's Dani's apartment.*

Did they let her go already? He doubted it. But why else would someone be inside?

If it was Dani, why would she have a light on? Not only would it waste batteries, but she knew announcing her presence was dangerous. It was an open invitation to every potential thief and rapist across the city. Not that Colt has seen many of them out and about, but still.

He unzipped the day pack and pulled out a pair of binoculars. Bringing them into focus while he stared at the apartment, Colt spotted an X in the window. He pulled the binoculars down.

The first thing he thought of was *The X-Files* and how Mulder taped an X in the window when he needed help. Dani loved the show almost as much as he did. It couldn't be a coincidence.

Did she need help?

Colt brought the binoculars back up as a shadow passed in front of the glass. A man wearing army green. *Shit.* He walked back and forth like an officer on the parade deck, waiting to catch a boot enlisted man out of line. From the stance and weight and the way his arms were held behind his back, it could only be one man: Colonel Jarvis.

What was he doing inside Dani's apartment? Colt kept watching, waiting for some sign of her. As he was about to give up, he spotted a little head in the window. A kid's head.

Dani.

Shoving the binoculars back in his bag, Colt made a decision. He would find out exactly what the army was up to, why they wanted him dead, and just what the hell was going on up there in Dani's apartment.

If she was in trouble, he would rescue her. It didn't matter that she'd told him goodbye. He wouldn't break his promise.

CHAPTER TWENTY-FIVE

COLT

55 HOUGHTON STREET, APARTMENT 409
Eugene, Oregon
9:00 p.m.

IT TOOK COLT OVER TWO HOURS TO FIND A SUITABLE lookout, clear it, and set up his gear. But now he sat in the darkness, staring across the street at Dani's apartment. The place glowed.

From his position about ten feet back from the window, Colt could see everything inside with his binoculars. Dani stayed curled up in the papasan chair in the corner underneath a blanket. He couldn't tell if she was sleeping or not, but at least the soldiers left her alone.

Two young enlisted guys sat at the table, constantly pointing at pieces of paper spread across it and intermittently using handheld radios. Another soldier stood guard by the door.

The colonel paced. His presence surprised Colt. The man was in charge of the entire unit. Why he would take it upon himself to accompany Dani to the apartment, Colt didn't have a clue. But he might be able to find out.

He picked up the handheld radio he'd stolen from the driver of the truck and turned it on. As long as he didn't say anything, they wouldn't know he was listening. He turned up the volume and waited.

"Echo 6 Romeo to Echo 7, radio check, over."

Colt sat a bit straighter in the chair.

"Echo 7, copy. Ready and waiting instructions."

"Proceed with house-by-house clearing in sector eight, nine, and ten. Transport all confiscated weapons and supplies to the loading bay. Over."

"Request for clarification, Echo 6. If we encounter hostiles what is the protocol?"

The radio crackled.

"All hostiles are to be eliminated on sight. No prisoners are authorized. Over."

Colt blinked. It was true. They were going house to house like the woman from the street had said. Was there some rival gang? Were they trying to protect the town from criminals?

If they were fighting an opposing force, Colt could help. He didn't need to be shot at. He wasn't a bad guy. Maybe the sporting goods store had been one colossal misunderstanding. If that were true…

The radio crackled again. "Echo 7 to Echo 6

Romeo, request permission to speak with Echo 6. Over."

Colt watched through his binoculars as one of the soldiers from the table stood up and walked over to Colonel Jarvis. He handed him the radio and the colonel brought it to his lips. "Echo 6."

"Sir…" Muffled sounds of an argument filtered through the radio. "Sir, this is Sergeant Gunther and I know we aren't supposed to question our orders, but these are residential sectors, sir."

The colonel resumed his pacing. "Your point, Gunther?"

"These people deserve our protection, sir. If we drag them out of their houses in the middle of the night, how are we earning their trust?"

Colt pressed the binoculars so hard against his face the plastic dug into his eye sockets. They couldn't be doing what it sounded like. Rounding up innocent civilians? The orders to kill couldn't have been about civilian protesters, could they? It didn't make sense.

The colonel spoke up. "How old are you, Sergeant Gunther?"

"Twenty-two, sir."

"Do you want to live to be twenty-three?"

"Yes, sir."

"Then you will kill every person who so much as looks at you funny out on that patrol. This isn't about giving anyone protection or earning their trust. It's about control. We own this town now and everything in it. If they want to stay alive, then they'll do it under our good graces. Nothing more. Is that understood?"

"Yes, sir."

The colonel handed the radio back to the other soldier and the man clicked it on. "Echo 6 Romeo to Echo 7, are your orders clear?"

"Yes. House-by-house clearing in sections eight, nine, and ten. Shoot hostiles on sight. Confiscate all weapons and critical supplies. Over."

The radio fell silent and Colt rocked back. He might as well have been clocked upside the head with a baseball bat. The National Guard unit stationed at the University of Oregon wasn't part of the United States Army anymore. It had gone completely off protocol. They weren't here in Eugene, Oregon to protect the town or set up communications. They were here to turn the little town into their own private fiefdom.

At least that was Colonel Jarvis's plan.

The thought made Colt sick. How could the man do such a thing? He had to have close to twenty years in the service. Now he wanted to use that experience against the very people he swore to protect?

Women and children lived in this town. Men who never picked up a gun and who didn't know the first thing about defending themselves. How could Jarvis just declare the whole place part of his kingdom?

Colt brought the binoculars back up and stared into the apartment. The radio had gone silent, but Jarvis still paced back and forth. Could Dani have heard what they were planning? Was she pretending to sleep, but listening in?

If so, she knew the danger she was in. Even if her grandmother were receiving the best care at the university hospital, she had to know it wouldn't last. Men like this didn't do anything out of kindness. They took Dani and Dorris because they wanted something.

Colt frowned. They wanted him.

For whatever reason, Jarvis saw him as a threat. Maybe it was the fact he was a former SEAL or his causal questions about their unit that rubbed Jarvis the wrong way. If he was disarming ordinary civilians, it made sense to disarm Colt, too.

Now that he'd killed four of Jarvis's men…

He set the binoculars down. As long as Colt roamed the streets, Dani wouldn't be safe. They would use her to get to him. He had to get her out of that apartment before they moved her somewhere he couldn't penetrate.

Colt forced himself to stand and walked over to the dark kitchen. He pulled the first aid kit out of his pack and opened the bottle of pain pills. Four went down his throat along with a half a bottle of Gatorade. Screw staying off medicine. Colt needed to block the pain to do what had to be done.

Digging out the duct tape and another bandage, he stripped to his underwear and tore strips of the tape long enough to wrap around his leg. With the bandage on top of his stitches, Colt wrapped the duct tape around his thigh, securing the bandage and covering the entire wound.

It wouldn't be good for breathability, but if he blew a stitch, he wouldn't bleed out. After it was all over, he could treat the wound again. He popped another antibiotic and washed it down with the rest of the Gatorade before pulling out a few energy bars.

Colt ate them in systematic fashion, fueling his body for the grueling night ahead. After he finished, he turned his attention to the apartment he stood inside. It appeared to be another college student's place, full of things like used textbooks and dirty laundry. A college *boy's* apartment.

Thankfully for Colt, a guy's place would have everything he needed. After a few minutes of searching, he compiled his supplies. Colt spread it all out on the floor of the walk-in closet, stuffed a pair of towels beneath the door, and turned on a portable lantern.

It wouldn't take much to put the necessary equipment together, but Colt needed the light. He started with the matches, pulling the paper backs off the packs, each one from the same bar in Eugene. A dive, probably. He taped the lot of them to the bottom of three aerosol deodorant cans, duct taped them all together, and set the bundle aside.

Thanks to an apartment dweller who liked to play his fair share of college drinking games, Colt had a whole pile of ping pong balls. He cut the majority of them up into little pieces and shoved the bits into five he'd punctured with a knife. Wrapping aluminum foil around each one, he shoved a rolled-up wad of paper towels and a match into the hole left behind and smiled.

College kids always had the best supplies.

After collecting all the magazines from each of the M-4s he'd stolen from the army attackers and stuffing his cargo pants full of them, Colt assembled everything he made. He was still outnumbered. Four army men inside a locked apartment versus a former SEAL with a wounded leg.

It wasn't much of a contest. The only problem would be keeping Dani safe. He didn't know if he could take all of them out before she became a hostage, but he would have to try his best. Colt slung the daypack loaded with gear over his shoulder and stepped into the hall.

Time to play action hero.

CHAPTER TWENTY-SIX

DANI

52 Houghton Street, Apartment 310
Eugene, Oregon
11:00 p.m.

Dani thought the soldiers might never fall asleep. Were they hopped up on a stolen supply of Red Bull or using nicotine patches like the fentanyl one they gave her mom to stay awake?

Whatever it was, they seemed close to super human. Their failure to yawn or even think about a bed drove Dani insane. She tried not to sleep, but curled up in the oversized, round chair, she couldn't help it. When she woke up, it was quiet.

The only light came from a single glowing spot by the far windows. A cigarette. She waited until her eyes adjusted to the light. One of the younger soldiers.

He sat by the window, sticking his lit cigarette out

into the dark in between puffs. At least she had some confirmation he was human after all.

With only one of them awake, now was her chance. She knew there was one way out of that place. Colt picked the apartment for her, not just because of the view of the surrounding streets, but for its relative security. The metal door would withstand a million pounding feet, the concrete walls any type of fire.

Even if Colt saw the X in the window, he wouldn't be able to rescue her. And Dani needed to get out. She couldn't let them take her back to the college. Now that she knew they weren't in this to keep Eugene safe or help anyone but themselves, she couldn't let them use her.

Users never cared about the people they took advantage of, they only took and took and took until there was nothing left. She learned that the hard way. Dani sniffed as she thought about Gran. Her mother even managed to take her away in the end.

But Dani wouldn't let that beat her. She was stronger than that. Somewhere between getting caught by that soldier in the street and telling Colt goodbye, she realized she was stronger than she thought possible.

Colt had given her that strength. She would get out. She would warn him and together they would get away. Even if he didn't want to be her dad or even her friend, she would make sure he was far, far away from these thugs who claimed to be the good guys.

She owed him that and so much more.

Dani sucked in a breath and lifted her arms over her head, stretching like a cat coming alive from a nap.

There was only one way out of that apartment and she was going to use it.

As she pretended to come around, the soldier didn't move from the window. Dani sat up casually, rubbing at her face like she couldn't wake up.

After a moment, she cast a glance his way, settling on his cigarette light. "Hey!" she whisper-shouted in his direction.

"What?"

She bit her lip and glanced around, acting the embarrassed teen. "I've got to pee."

"Hold it."

"I can't, mister. I've gotta go real bad." Dani squirmed in the chair, crossing her legs one over the other. "I don't think the colonel wants to wake up to the smell of it all over this chair."

The soldier grumbled under his breath and Dani caught a few creative curses as he stubbed out his cigarette and stood up. "I'll get you a bottle of water, so you can use the toilet and flush with it."

"Thank you!" She bounced in the seat like she did when she was little, hopping up and down to make it clear she had to go.

As he retrieved the water, Dani wrapped the blanket around her shoulders, pretending to shiver in the already warm room. "What is it about having to pee that makes you so cold?" She bounced some more, adding in a stream of useless chatter as the soldier walked back to her.

She'd learned a long time ago the more a kid talked, the more a grown-up tuned her out. They didn't want to hear about the salamander you found one time in the backyard or the time some kid in your class broke his arm on the monkey bars.

He didn't say a word when he handed her the bottle or when she stood up with the blanket. "Thanks." She eyed the water and glanced at the hall. "It might take a minute. I've got to um… you know… do a little more than pee."

The soldier rolled his eyes. "Whatever. Just don't wake up the colonel. He'll be pissed."

"Good to know." Dani hustled into the bathroom and locked the door. She didn't have very long.

Tugging her clothes off her body, she tied one leg of her jeans to the corner of the blanket, pulling as hard as she could on the ends to ensure the knot would hold. Then she did the same thing with her shirt and sweatshirt, adding as much length to the makeshift rope as she could manage.

They were three floors off the ground. The longer the rope, the less risk of breaking her bones when she landed. She hoped the speck of grass below the window was as soft as it looked.

A knock sounded on the door and Dani jumped. "How's it going in there?"

"Um…" Dani glanced at the locked door. Would it hold if he tried to kick it down? *Probably not.* "I… ah… need a few minutes. Those meals you all keep feeding me aren't helping with the digestion, you know?"

He said something about getting used to it, but Dani wasn't listening. She relieved herself in the toilet and chugged the water, leaving her pee to stink up the bowl. *Serves the jerks right.*

With a deep breath she clambered in the tub and dragged the makeshift rope in with her. The window was one of those old crank types with a metal casing and a little lever that stuck up from the sill. She twisted it slowly to minimize the noise and opened the window as far as it would go. She would barely fit.

Tying a free corner of the blanket to the crank, she gave it a hard tug. Whether it would hold or not, she didn't know. But what choice did she have? Colt needed her. She had to get away.

The soldier knocked again. "Kid, come on. You can't still be taking a dump. Get out here."

Dani grabbed the bundle of blanket and clothes and began stuffing it through the window. "Sorry! I'll just be another minute!"

The handle jiggled. Dani worked faster shoving the fluffy thing through as the soldier worked the door.

"Open up! Right now!"

She ignored him, hoisting her body up to reach the window. It was a little too high. *No, no, no!* This can't be happening. She jumped again, ignoring the noise her feet made when they hit the tile.

This time she found purchase, pushing up with her arms until they locked, her palms flat on the sill. Grunting with effort, she lifted one leg and stuck her foot through the window.

She looked ridiculous. Any other time, if someone told her she'd be trying to escape through a third-story window wearing nothing but her bra, undies, and a pair of sneakers, she'd have thought they were as high as her mother. But emergencies did strange things to people.

Just as Dani came to rest, one leg in, one leg out of the window, the door slammed open. The soldier stumbled into the bathroom, leading with his shoulder.

Dani's eyes went wide and she ducked underneath the open pane, teetering on the edge of the sill. There wasn't a balcony. Just a wall of concrete and windows all the way down to the ground. If she slipped... If the blanket didn't hold...

Fear gripped her as the soldier clambered forward, rifle in one hand as he rushed to reach her. *Now or never.*

Dani grabbed the blanket, about to jump for it, when the soldier raised his gun. "Do it and I shoot. If the bullet doesn't kill you, the fall to the ground will."

She hesitated and it was all the soldier needed. He grabbed her by the ankle and yanked. Dani lost her balance. The only thing keeping her from falling was the soldier's sweaty hand.

She screamed as she fell forward, her face staring straight at the earth. Propelling her arms in frantic windmills, she searched for anything to hold onto. There was nothing.

The soldier grunted as he grabbed her again, his knobby fingers digging into her naked flesh.

His hands were on her calf, then thigh, then right around her middle. He dragged her back into the bathroom despite her struggling against him. The second her feet landed on the tub floor he caged her against the tile.

His breath hit hot on her face. "You thought you

could get away? That this little trick would set you free?" One of his hands found her throat, squeezing until she could barely breathe.

"Y-You're hurting me."

"That's the point." His other hand roved up and down her body, pausing to grope her breast before diving down between her legs.

"I thought you were just some stupid kid, but there's enough meat on your bones." His fingers were thick and stubby and Dani scrabbled at his hand.

"Stop it!" She tried to scream again, but the soldier only tightened his grip on her throat.

He leered, his face so close she could see his pores. "They won't come to help you. Hell, the other two can't stop talking about what they're gonna do with you once the colonel gets what he wants." His hand dug between her thighs, fingernails scratching her skin. "I told them they were nuts, but now..." He licked his lips. "I bet you'd feel real nice. You want a soldier for your first time?"

He grabbed at his belt as Dani's vision dimmed. He gripped her throat so hard she couldn't breathe. Blood whooshed in her ears like a chorus of cicadas.

Help! Help me! She flailed her arms, palm landing haphazardly against the shower walls. It was no use. She sagged against the cold tile.

Dani thought about Colt, and what they would do to him when they found him. *Colt.*

Strong and capable. Able to fight off how many men at once? Dani shuddered. Feet. Groin. *Eyes. I remember!*

She made spears out of her index and middle fingers. Steeled her courage.

I can do this.

The soldier cursed as his belt gave him difficulty and he tore his gaze away from her face to look at the buckle. His grip on her throat relaxed as he concentrated. It was the only chance she would get.

Dani sucked in as much air as she could and lashed out, her fingers diving straight for the soldier's eyes. She screamed as her fingertips made contact and kept going, jabbing into his eyeballs like spoons into set Jell-O.

On and on she pushed, the moment stretching out like it could go on forever. His blood coated her fingers, his eyeballs gushed and Dani didn't stop. She channeled all of her anger—at her mother, the death of Gran, the lies the soldiers told, all of it—into her force and rage.

The soldier screamed, a high-pitched whine of terror, and released her. He fell to the floor of the tub, his face covered in blood, his eyes no longer functional.

As Dani lunged for the soldier's rifle, a massive explosion shook the entire building and she fell on top of the wounded man.

CHAPTER TWENTY-SEVEN

COLT

52 HOUGHTON STREET, THIRD FLOOR HALLWAY
Eugene, Oregon
11:30 p.m.

COLT SET THE THREE-PACK OF AEROSOL CANS ON THE
floor outside the metal apartment door. When he'd
picked out the place for Dani, he'd been impressed with
how secure it had been. Now he was cursing that same
security. He didn't know if the aerosol bomb would blow
the door, but it was his best bet.

He needed to rescue Dani and put as many miles
between them and the army-turned-militia as he could.
Colt crouched in front of the door and flicked the spark
wheel on a lighter. Holding the flame to the bundles of
matches taped to the bottom of the cans, he waited until
a good portion were lit before stepping back.

Ducking behind the corner, he took aim with the M-

4. A single burst should do the trick. He inhaled, held his breath, and fired. The cans exploded in an instant. A huge fireball whooshed up the door.

The floors rumbled, the walls shook, and the metal door burst open. *Bingo*.

Colt grabbed the aluminum-wrapped ping pong balls and held the lighter to the paper and match wicks one at a time. As soon as each began to smoke, he tossed them into the apartment.

Noxious smoke filled the air and Colt crouched low to the ground, waiting.

Shouts erupted inside. A girl's scream. *Dani*.

He advanced, hugging the wall to keep his back covered, bandana tied around his face to keep some of the smoke out of his lungs. *Get Dani and get out.* That's all he needed to do.

The smoke filled the apartment, but it would dissipate soon. He scanned the space, creeping along the edges, swinging his rifle back and forth in slow arcs as he crouch-walked along the wall. Into the kitchen, around the table where he'd seen them working. *Empty*.

Out of the kitchen and into the living room. The smoke began to ease. More shouts. More screaming. All the activity came from the bedroom and bathroom.

Goosebumps broke out on his arms. They wouldn't hurt her… would they?

"Dani!" He shouted despite his instincts telling him to stay quiet. "Dani!"

A volley of gunfire erupted from the hallway. Colt dove for the couch, fumbling along the ground as he sought cover. Bullets slammed into the couch, spraying little bursts of feathers into the air. More bullets sailed over his head, hitting the windows and shattering the glass.

The building was too old for tempered glass, so it fell in massive, jagged sheets, clattering to the ground and dumping fresh air into the room. Colt ripped off the bandana and gulped down some air.

"Dani!"

She screamed again and Colt steeled himself for a battle. He had to reach her.

He rose up as the last of the smoke cleared. No soldiers lurked in his field of vision; they had all retreated to the bedroom. He couldn't rush them; he would be dead before he made it five feet. They couldn't leave without walking right by him.

Colt cursed. It was a stalemate.

Flushing the soldiers out was the only option. Colt thought about what he could do, glancing around the living room for anything he could use. Couch riddled with bullets. Rolled-up rug. Papasan chair. Bookcase.

He rushed to the shelves and grabbed as many books as he could in one load and tossed them on the floor at the foot of the couch. The soldiers were quiet. Too quiet.

Either they were coming up with a plan or they were about to attack. He didn't have much time. Colt grabbed the ottoman to the papasan chair and looped an arm through an opening before pilling books on top. With the M-4 pressed tight against his shoulder and ready to fire, he stood and rushed into the kitchen.

No shots.

He grabbed the spray oil he'd seen the other day and ripped pages from the books, balling them up into tennis ball-sized bundles before spraying each one with oil. He soaked the pages of each ball until they dripped and nestled them all into the cushion of the ottoman.

With his lighter, he lit each ball, building a burning inferno. He grabbed the kitchen cart tucked into the corner and tipped it over, throwing the utensils and useless kitchen gear out of the way.

Colt set the ottoman on top and waited for the cushion and balsam wood to light. As soon as the wood caught fire, the flames leaped into the air, singeing the ceiling and gusting upward.

He rolled the cart by pushing it with the barrel of the rifle. Out of the kitchen he nudged it, until it sat at the entrance to the hall. He knew he was risking Dani's life with what he was about to do, but Colt didn't see another choice.

The soldiers wouldn't come out unless they had to. With a good kick he sent the kitchen cart rolling down the hall to the closed bedroom door. It slammed into the wood and the flames rose, curling around the door and lighting the trim on fire.

Colt brought the bandana back up to his face and rushed down the hall to the bathroom. He ducked inside as smoke filled the hall.

The first thing he saw was the blood. So much blood. The window stood open and something soft and fuzzy hung on the crank. Colt stepped around the worst of the spatter and climbed into the tub.

A blanket was tied to the window crank. Colt leaned over the edge of the window and caught sight of it fluttering in the breeze. His eyes widened.

He would recognize that sweatshirt anywhere. *Dani.* She had tried to escape. He spun back around, stared at the blood. If he was too late... If that blood was hers...

Colt cupped his hand around his mouth. "It's over, Jarvis. Come out and I won't shoot."

The door had to be just about burned through. The flames licked up the hallway, cruising toward the bathroom and the wood trim. In minutes, Colt would be trapped. The soldiers and Dani already were.

He leaned out the window, trying to see into the bedroom. The windows there were open, too, letting in air to breathe but also feeding the fire with fresh oxygen.

If they didn't move soon, they would die in there.

All at once, a massive crash rocked the apartment. Sparks flew into the hall. Screaming that could only be Dani's began. Colt stood up, prepared to rush into the flames. He climbed over the edge of the tub and eased toward the hall.

As he stuck his head out, a huge piece of ceiling fell, crashing to the ground between him and the bedroom.

Dani screamed again and Colt finally saw her. She stood just inside the bedroom wearing nothing but a bra and underwear. Seeing her like that broke something inside Colt. She wasn't just a girl he'd helped for a few days before he left town.

She was funny and kind and despite all the hell she'd been through as a kid, she still let him in. Dani was the closest to a daughter he would ever have and he couldn't let her down. If they survived, he would ask her to be a part of his family. He would ask her to stay.

She screamed and Colt bit back the urge to rush in and save her. It's exactly what they wanted. He stared at her, heart aching in his chest. *Just run, Dani. Just take a chance and run to me.*

Colt waved his arms and she looked up, fear and panic ringing her pupils in white. She shook her head violently back and forth, screaming and flailing her hands. Someone shoved her in the back and she stumbled toward the fire.

Come on, kid. You can do this. Take a chance and run.

He brought his hands up in an X-shape, hoping she would see him through the smoke and the flames and understand. She turned to look behind her as another piece of the ceiling fell.

It was now or never. *Run or I'm coming to get you.*

He knew that was what the soldiers wanted. They never expected her to take such a big risk. But Colt trusted Dani. He trusted her strength and courage and ability to survive. He put his arms up in an X again, letting go of the rifle, begging her to trust him.

She spun back around and her face changed. Her jaw locked and she nodded. *Yes!*

Squeezing her eyes shut and bracing against the flames, Dani took off. She ran straight into the fire and straight toward Colt. The soldiers shouted. She kept coming.

A lick of flames caught her hair and lapped against her bare skin, but she didn't stop.

Colt caught her in his arms and dragged her into the bathroom as gunfire once again erupted. He grunted when a bullet hit his arm, but he didn't stop. Another grazed his head, but Colt ignored it. They crashed into the bathroom, landing hard on the tile floor still slick with blood.

Colt grabbed the hand towel still on the wall and batted at Dani's head, putting out the fire smoldering in her hair. As soon as it stopped burning, he tossed the towel aside and grabbed her by the shoulders.

"Dani! Dani are you all right?"

She shook uncontrollably, sobbing and unable to speak.

Damn it. Colt hauled her into the bathtub and climbed in with her, slipping in the blood only half-congealed inside the tub. He forced Dani down into the cold tub basin, and brought up his rifle. Jarvis wouldn't take them alive.

A volley of shots flew into the bathroom. At least two shooters firing in three-round bursts as fast as their M-4s could manage. Colt ducked, covering Dani with as much of his body as he could.

The soldiers shouted and the bullets kept coming. Flames licked the walls of the bathroom, catching the towels and paper products on fire.

They didn't have long.

Soldiers shouted. "Get out! Get out!"

"What about them?"

"If they aren't dead, they will be. Go! Go!"

More bullets. Colt squeezed down tight over Dani, absorbing her shakes as he prayed.

CHAPTER TWENTY-EIGHT

DANI

52 HOUGHTON STREET, APARTMENT 310
Eugene, Oregon
12:15 a.m.

COLT'S TWO HUNDRED POUNDS PRESSED DOWN ON TOP of Dani and she struggled to breathe. He still held her in the bathtub, but the soldiers had stopped shooting. It had all happened so fast.

She was suffocating in there, with his body weight pressing down on top of her and the smoke filling the room. They had to get out.

She smacked her dry lips together, tried to get her aching throat to work. "Colt?"

He rose up a fraction.

"Are they gone?"

"If they aren't dead, then, yes." His weight lifted and Dani sucked in a breath, coughing instead of breathing.

"We... we need to get out of here."

"The fire is too thick. We have to wait it out."

Dani sat up and smoke swirled around her head. "We can't. We'll suffocate."

Colt choked on a cough and pointed at the open window. "How far did you get?"

"Halfway. If I'd been a little quicker, I'd have gotten out."

He rose up in the tub, shielding his face as he tested the window. "Stand up and I'll hoist you out."

Dani blinked the tears out of her eyes caused by the smoke. "I want you to go first. If I fall, you can catch me."

Colt coughed again. "I can't fit through the window, Dani."

She pushed herself up to stand. "Then break it."

"Even if I break it, I don't think I can get up there. It's pretty high."

Dani glanced down at her body. Dried blood covered her hands and arms, soot coated everything else, and her head ached from the burns. The second the flames singed her scalp, she thought that was it. No way would she make it.

A teenage girl running through fire in nothing but a pair of sneakers and her underwear? Right. Movies were made of less. But she did make it. And now Colt wanted to give up?

She glared at him, the shakes and the fear replaced by anger. "So that's it? You risk your life to get in here, blow the door off its hinges, set everything on fire, and a little window is going to stop you?"

Colt scowled. "I won't be much good to you with my brains splattered all over the pavement."

She snorted. "There's grass down there. It will cushion your fall." Dani reached out and took his hand. "I have faith in you, Colt. You'll make it. You can do anything."

He broke eye contact and stepped out of the tub. "Better get behind me. This will be messy."

Dani climbed over the edge of the tub, cowering between Colt, the toilet, and the flames. He aimed the rifle at the window and fired enough shots to turn it into a million little pieces.

"Watch the glass." Colt cranked the window shut, trapping the blanket between the frame and the sill. He shifted his rifle to hang over his shoulder and with a deep breath, used his arms to hoist himself up.

His left arm wobbled, buckling as he came close to level, but he managed to hold on enough to get his butt up on the ledge. His face contorted in pain.

"Are you all right?"

"I'll live." He glanced out the window. "Assuming I survive the fall."

Dani eased back over to the window, side-stepping the biggest hunks of glass. "I'll be right behind you."

Colt nodded and stuck his head out before swinging his legs over the sill. He grabbed the blanket and tested the knot. "Good tying."

She smiled, but it was short-lived. What if he was right? What if the blanket didn't hold him or he slipped and fell the three stories to the ground? Dani would watch him die.

"Colt!" His name came out tortured and raw. "Be careful."

With another nod, he twisted, sliding out of the window and disappearing from view. "Colt!" Dani screamed this time, leaping up against the tile and scrabbling with her feet for purchase. She cut her hand on a shard of glass but didn't care. Forcing her arms to support her weight, she hoisted herself into the open window.

Colt waved to her from about a story down and Dani's heart eased out of her throat. "I thought you fell!"

"Not yet."

He reached the end of the makeshift rope and glanced at the ground. Dani swallowed. It was still so far.

"Maybe you shouldn't watch."

"No. I want to. I know you'll make it."

Colt closed his eyes and let go. He landed hard on the grassy strip below the window, rolling over as his feet touched the ground. He didn't get up.

"Colt!" Dani stuck her head out the window and gripped the top as she swung her legs over and into the air. She had to get to him.

Dani grabbed the blanket and turned around. *I can do this. I have to do this.*

She pushed herself off the window, wobbling as her feet slid on the side of the building. With her arms taut and fingers digging into the fabric, Dani walked down the wall, inch by inch.

Without the heat from the fire, the cold air chilled

her bare skin and she shivered. When she reached the end of the rope, her fingers wrapped around her sweatshirt as she dangled still so far from the ground.

Colt groaned.

She twisted in the air to catch a glimpse of him. "Are you okay?"

"I might have broken something."

Oh, no. "But you're breathing."

"Yeah."

Okay. This will be okay. All she had to do was jump. Dani climbed back up higher on the rope and wrapped her arm with one of the legs of her jeans. Once she felt secure, she worked on the knot between her sweatshirt and T-shirt, tugging with one hand and her teeth until it loosened.

Whether her fall was two feet higher or lower, she figured it probably didn't matter. She'd rather have something to wear. After pulling the sweatshirt free, Dani clutched it to her chest.

A whoosh of heat from up above caught her attention and she glanced up. The flames were in the bathroom. Any minute, they would catch the blanket. She had to go. Now.

As she prepared to drop, Colt hoisted himself up to stand, using the rifle as a crutch. "When you jump, try to slow your fall. Grab the wall or a ledge. Anything."

Dani nodded. "If I don't?"

"Bend your knees and let your feet take the impact."

She glanced back up. The flames were thicker. Hotter. She took a deep breath and thought of Gran before she let go.

It wasn't like you see on TV. No slow-motion, life flashing before her eyes, fingers reaching out like a snail to grab the wall. *No.*

The ground rose up like a tidal wave, hard and fast, and slammed into her with brutal force. Her feet took most of the impact, legs buckling as gravity dragged her down. Dani fell onto her side, bouncing before she came to a stop.

Colt limped over to her. "Dani! Are you all right?"

She groaned and rolled over. "Yeah." She sat up, wincing as the shock of the fall still worked through her body. After tugging the sweatshirt over her head, she stood on shaky legs. "Can you walk?"

"Sort of."

"I can help." Dani reached out and grabbed Colt by the arm, supporting some of his weight as he struggled. The man was so big. She grunted and collapsed a bit, but managed not to fall. "Where to?"

He grimaced and took a step toward the street. "My gear is in there." Colt pointed to a building fifty feet away.

"Can you make it?"

"Don't have much of a choice."

Colt took another step and Dani came with him, supporting him as best she could. Together they had to be quite a sight: a hulk of man dressed all in black clutching a teenage girl wearing nothing but an oversized hoodie.

Dani struggled beneath Colt's weight, breaking out in a sweat despite the cool night air. After what seemed like hours, they made it inside the building. Colt leaned against the wall, sweat covering his face and dripping off his nose.

Dani glanced at the front door. "How long do you think we can stay here? Won't they be coming soon?"

He nodded. "We don't have much time. Let's go." He resumed his tortured pace, struggling up each stair as he practically hung off the rail.

They made it to the top floor and he fished out keys. "It's apartment 410. All the way down the hall. Unlock it and dig out a first aid kit. Alcohol from the kitchen, too."

Dani rushed down the hall without looking back. The key turned in the lock and she made it inside before heading straight for the kitchen. She grabbed a bottle of vodka before fishing the first aid kit out of a backpack on the floor. By the time she opened it up, Colt made his way into the apartment and shut the door.

"What do we do now?"

Colt sagged to the floor. "Now you open up that vodka, find a pair of tweezers, and dig this bullet out of my arm."

Dani stared. "You're joking right?"

Colt reached for his shirt and gave it a yank, tearing it just above the swell of his bicep. A hole in his upper arm oozed blood.

"Is that?"

"A gunshot wound? Yeah." He reached up and felt his head, pulling away sticky red fingers. "Lucky for me the other one only grazed my head."

Dani rushed over, staring in disbelief at his arm. "You really want me to fish around in there?"

He nodded. "If you don't, I'll probably die."

Crap.

She glanced at the bottle in her hands. "Do I pour this on the wound?"

"No. You hand it to me so I can drink it."

DAY NINETEEN

CHAPTER TWENTY-NINE

DANI

55 Houghton Street, Apartment 409
Eugene, Oregon
2:00 a.m.

The tweezers slipped and Colt grunted in pain. "Sorry."

"It's okay. Just try not to do that again."

Dani nodded and focused again on the bullet hole in Colt's arm. She eased the tweezers back inside and felt around for the bullet. "I can't find it. Are you sure it's in there?"

Colt's face paled the more she worked. "There's no exit wound, so unless I've turned into a worthless version of Wolverine and fused the lead to my bones, yeah. It's in there."

Dani let the criticism go. She knew he had to be in agony. With a deep breath, she tried again.

The tweezers hit something. "I think I found it." She hesitated. "Unless that's your bone. Please tell me that's not your bone."

"It's the bullet. Pull it out."

Dani did as Colt asked, first opening the tweezers then sliding them around the hunk of metal. It slipped. "Sorry."

He didn't respond.

She grabbed a hold of the bullet again and with a slow, steady movement, pulled it from his arm. Colt held out a shaking hand and she dropped the bloody hunk into his waiting palm.

He turned it over, inspecting it before leaning his head back against the wall. "It's all there." He took another swig of the vodka before handing it to her. "Now you can pour this on the wound."

Dani took the bottle and did as Colt asked, pouring a couple glugs of the liquor straight onto the hole in his arm.

He grimaced, but managed to point at the first aid kit. "Slap a bandage on it, will you? I've got to wrap my ankle."

While Dani applied a bandage to Colt's bicep, he pulled up his pant leg.

She paused. "Is that duct tape?"

He nodded. "Stab wound. I sewed it up, but I think the fall popped a stitch." He poked at the tape. "I'll have to deal with it later."

"When were you stabbed?"

He glanced at his watch. "Yesterday."

"Was it army guys? Four of them?"

He nodded.

"Did you kill them?"

Colt nodded again and Dani reeled. "So it's true? You ambushed those men and took them out?"

"What? No. Who told you that?"

"Colonel Jarvis. He said they were after you because you killed four of his men. Ambushed them and took them out for no reason whatsoever."

Colt snorted. "He would say that."

"It's not true?"

"Try the other way around. I'd just left a sporting goods store—the place I found all this gear—when they ambushed me. Trapped me in the loading bay. I tried to tell them who I was and not to shoot, but they didn't care." Colt rubbed his beard. "It was them or me, Dani. You have to believe that."

Dani rocked back on her heels and sat on the floor. "I believe you." Colt never gave her a reason to doubt his sincerity. The army, however, had done plenty to erode her trust. Every last bit of it. She tugged on the hem of her sweatshirt to cover her bare legs.

Colt motioned toward the pack. "I've got a pair of pants in there you can put on. One of the legs is ripped off above the knee. If you do the same with the other side, you'll have some long shorts."

She nodded and dug through his pack before pulling out the pants. After cutting off the full leg to match the other, she pulled them on. They fell right off.

Dani laughed and her throat threatened to close up, partly from the smoke inhalation during the fire and partly from exhaustion and too many emotions she struggled to keep in check.

"Dani."

She didn't look up.

"Dani, look at me."

She risked a quick glance.

"Are you okay? They didn't…" Colt struggled with the words. "When I found you, you didn't have any clothes on. They didn't hurt you, did they?"

Dani shook her head. "No. I locked myself in the bathroom once I decided to escape. The blanket wasn't long enough, so I used my clothes to extend it as far as I could." She grabbed the too-big pants and sat down. "I was halfway through the window when a soldier broke through the bathroom door."

Colt waited for a moment before asking what she hoped he wouldn't. "What happened?"

She shrugged and grabbed at the tie to her sweatshirt, pulling it through the hood as she replied. If she focused on the task, she wouldn't have to look him in the eye. "I was in my underwear and he grabbed me around the throat. Shoved me up against the shower wall." Her fingers shook, but she still managed to feed the tie through the belt loops on the pants, one by one. "At first I panicked, but then…"

She risked a glance up at Colt. He looked at her with such compassion and patience.

He didn't make her feel ashamed or afraid. He was a good man. "You fought back?"

Dani nodded and went back to working on the makeshift belt. She tied it around her waist as she answered. "I used my fingers just like you showed me, two spears. I… I gouged out his eyes."

Saying it out loud made it so very real. Dani couldn't believe what she had done. She chewed on her lip and focused on the floor.

After a moment, Colt exhaled. "Good job, Dani. I'm proud of you."

Her eyes flicked up. "You are?"

Colt nodded. "It takes real courage to do what you did. And to run through that fire. You're a survivor, that's for damn sure."

She smiled under the weight of his praise. No one but Gran had ever complimented her before. *Gran.* Dani's heart ached at the loss. "Gran's dead."

Colt blinked. "I'm sorry."

She nodded back tears. "Thanks." She had to change the subject. Enough hashing over the past. "How can I help with your leg?"

"Grab me two magazines from the table and the duct tape."

After she returned with both, Dani watched while Colt rolled the magazines into a pair of tubes and taped them to his ankle. After he finished, he pushed up to stand and test it out.

"Will it work?"

He shrugged. "Don't have much of a choice. Let's grab the gear and go. We need to get out of Eugene."

* * *

Streets of Eugene, Oregon

5:00 a.m.

COLT STUMBLED AND FELL TO ONE KNEE AND DANI bent down to drag him back up to his feet. "I think we should stop."

"No." Colt's single word came out in a growl, the pain of his injuries turning the man into a stumbling, monosyllabic mess.

Dani didn't know how much longer she could support his weight. He'd been so optimistic when they left the apartment, but he underestimated his injuries. Half-carrying him for miles took its toll. Every time Colt stumbled and Dani kept him upright, her back screamed. Pretty soon both of them would collapse.

She looked around her. They were in a residential neighborhood. From the looks of the quiet, shuttered houses, the army had already cleared this sector. That meant they weren't safe. No one would help them here.

Wrapping her arm around Colt's waist, Dani helped him walk.

They made it another twenty feet until he fell, face first, onto the sidewalk. Dani slammed her hands over her mouth to keep from screaming.

She crouched beside him, yanking on his arm. "Colt! Colt, you have to get up!"

It was no use. Colt was unconscious.

She kneeled on the ground and smacked his face, her open palm as loud as a gunshot in the silence. Colt didn't move. Dani didn't know what to do. She bent closer to his ear. "Colt, please. You have to get up." She tugged on his arm again. *Nothing.*

Dragging herself up, she approached the nearest house, a little bungalow with bright yellow paint and daisies out front. She took the front steps two at a time and knocked on the door. "Hello? Hello? Is anyone there? My friend needs help. Hello?"

She leaned back to look at the second story, but not a single curtain moved. *Crap.* She tried the next house, another two-story with a rocking chair on the front porch and a welcome sign by the door. *No answer.*

The next and the next and the next were the same. Either the street was abandoned, or no one was willing to help. No one would take the chance.

Dani ran back to Colt. She beat on his back. "Wake up! You can't freaking quit on me. Everyone else in my life has quit on me. You're not going to, do you hear me?" Her words turned to sobs. "Please, just get up."

The sound of a car engine filtered through the houses and Dani lurched to her feet. She grabbed Colt by the arms and tugged. He moved an inch. She pulled again, but it was no use.

Two hundred pounds of dead weight were impossible to move. After all they had been through. After everything they survived that night, they would be captured.

She thought about the soldier in the bathroom and her hands went to her neck.

"Hey!"

Dani spun around, her eyes wide with the fear at

what might be coming. An older man stood across the street. He waved. "Are you with him?" He pointed at Colt.

"Yes." She hesitated, but what choice did she have? She had to trust him. She looked at Colt. "He's unconscious. I can't move him."

The man crossed the street and bent to check Colt's pulse. "He's still alive. Let's flip him over. I'll grab one arm, you grab the other. We can drag him into my cellar." The engine noise increased as the man flipped Colt onto his back. "We need to hurry."

With the stranger helping, Dani managed to pull Colt across the road and into the side yard between two buildings. As they eased into the shadows, headlights lit up the street.

"Hurry. Down here." The man motioned to a pair of open storm doors. He went first, holding up Colt's torso, and Dani picked up Colt's feet. Her head disappeared below the opening as the headlights lit up the house.

The second the lights disappeared, the stranger reached up and shut the cellar doors.

DAY TWENTY-ONE

CHAPTER THIRTY

COLT

Basement, Location Unknown
Eugene, Oregon
9:00 p.m.

Colt groaned and twisted onto his side, but pain in his arm forced him back. His hands rubbed over soft sheets and he blinked. *Where am I?*

The last thing he remembered was trudging through the night with Dani at his side, every step more painful than the last. He tried to sit up and a familiar voice spoke up.

"Hey, stranger."

Colt opened his eyes and a pretty young girl came into focus. Light brown hair cut short in a pixie style, bright brown eyes open wide. A smile that would light up the darkest room. "Dani?"

She smiled even wider. "Hey, Colt."

He struggled to sit up. They were in a bedroom with a pair of twin beds and a small nightstand between them. A little lantern lit up the space. "Where are we?"

"Mr. Wilkins' basement."

"And that would be where?"

She exhaled. "Inside the army's cleared zone. We've been safe so far, but it's touch and go. Now that you're awake, we can talk about options."

Colt shook his head. "I don't understand."

Dani smiled again. "You've been asleep for almost two days."

Damn. Colt glanced down at his arm. The bandage had been changed. He pulled back the covers to reveal a clean T-shirt, shorts, and a leg free of duct tape. A fresh bandage covered the knife wound. "Who's helping us?"

"They call themselves the Resistance." She almost giggled. "If you think you can walk, you can see for yourself. It's just about time for the nightly meeting."

Colt twisted in the bed and reached for a pair of folded-up pants. He slid them up over his tender ankle and bandaged leg and managed to stand without collapsing. Dani helped him to the door. "You're sure they're trustworthy?"

She nodded. "Come on. You'll see."

Together, they hobbled out into a basement living room. Six people turned and stood at the sound of their approach. Colt took in their faces. A pair of men in their early thirties. A woman of fifty, maybe older. A young man who couldn't have much older than Dani.

Colt paused at a woman holding a little brown and gray dog. "Melody?"

"Hi, Colt."

Dani glanced up at him. "You know each other?"

Colt rubbed the back of his neck. "We met on the street after the ambush. She was nice enough to talk to me. She told me the truth about the army's activity here."

Melody nodded. "It's good to see you up on your feet." She held one hand out to the man standing beside her. "This is Harvey Wilkins. It's his house we're in."

Colt turned to the man and paused. He was older, maybe mid-sixties, with thinning gray hair and a patient expression. Something in Colt's memory caught and he tried to place it. "I'm sorry, have we met?"

"Only in passing. I own a book shop across from the sporting goods store."

The memory clicked. "You were there when the ambush happened. I saw you standing across the street, watching."

Harvey held out his hand. "Yes, that was me. When I saw you in the street here, I knew you were one of the good guys. I helped Danielle get you inside."

Colt glanced at her and mouthed, *Danielle?*

She shrugged, smiling. It seemed like so much had happened since he'd been unconscious. "Thank you all for helping us. I don't know what we would have done without your generosity."

Harvey nodded. "You're welcome, but it's not all altruistic. We're hoping once you're well, that you can help us."

"With the army?"

"Yes. We have to do something. They're still clearing sectors of town, but it won't be long before they've finished. Then what will happen? Work camps? Raids? They won't let us stay in our homes forever." Harvey glanced around at the group of people assembled. "We won't let them take everything from us. It isn't right."

Colt turned to Dani. He'd always thought that if something like this happened, he would disappear, turn into a nomad and live in the backcountry all on his own. No one to care about but himself, no hard choices.

But she changed him. He didn't want to leave her here and set off with nothing but a pack and his wits. He wanted to protect her, keep her safe, watch her grow into the adult he knew she could be. Colt reached out and took her hand.

She squeezed.

"Going up against a group like this won't be easy. They're well-trained, follow orders, heavily armed. They won't go down without a fight."

"We know. That's why we need your help."

Colt didn't know what to say. How could this little group of civilians ever hope to go against an organized militia? Colt could help, but not enough.

The boy close to Dani's age spoke up. "Grandad, it's about time. Can I turn it on?'

"Sure, Will." The boy rushed to the coffee table and kneeled in front of it. A little radio sat on the tabletop with a cord running up the wall. At first Colt thought it was power, but when he saw the kid crank a lever on the side of the radio, he realized it was an antenna.

Will twisted a knob and leaned back, waiting. All of the locals went back to their spots in chairs and the couch. Dani tugged on Colt's hand. They walked over and Colt sat in an overstuffed chair, Dani on the arm.

The radio crackled to life. "Good evening. The time is nine thirty Pacific Standard, and it has been twenty-one days since the United States power grid failed. My name is Walter Sloane."

Colt stared at the radio. The pilot from the plane? *It can't be.*

"I'm broadcasting again this evening to give everyone listening hope. Although we are facing the toughest ordeal our country has had to face in over a generation, we will survive. Everyone listening tonight has the ability to weather this storm.

"Wherever you are, start preparing. Stop looking for the government or the military or anyone else to help you. The best person to help right now is you. Look around you. Find friends and neighbors you can trust. People who want to beat these odds. Don't let adversity stop you."

Colt leaned back in the chair. The voice was indeed that of Walter Sloane, the pilot who emergency-landed the 747 that brought him to Eugene, Oregon. He'd made it. Wherever he was broadcasting from, the man had survived.

Walter kept speaking about the future, how to prepare, what needed to be done to survive. The more he talked, the more Colt knew the man was right. This wasn't a time to go off on his own. Even if he could convince Dani to come with him, how long would they last out there in the wild? A year? More? At some point, they would have to stop running. They would need to settle down.

Colt had been around enough; he'd experienced enough of life to know he could survive without a wife or a lover or even friends. He glanced at Dani. She was only fifteen. All of that was still ahead of her. He couldn't ask her to give it all up.

Not if he didn't have to. Colt turned back to the radio.

"Assemble the basics. Water. Food. Shelter. But go beyond that. Find a favorite book. A treasured necklace. A picture your kid made before the world fell apart. Make it your talisman. Hold onto it. Remember our life the way it was before.

"Not the video games and the 24/7 news and the never-ending quest for escape. But the little things. The simpler things we can all get back to. That's how you'll stay human. That's how you'll survive.

"This great country of ours will rebuild. This isn't the end of us and it isn't the end of you. Have faith. Until tomorrow, this is Walter Sloane, saying goodnight and good luck."

The radio fell silent and Colt looked up. Harvey sat in a chair opposite Colt, watching him.

"How long has Walter been broadcasting?"

Harvey glanced at the radio. "Only a few days. Why?"

"He was the pilot who landed my plane."

Everyone in the room turned to look at Colt. Will, the teenager, spoke up. "You know him?"

Colt nodded. "Last I saw of him, he was headed to Sacramento to find his wife and daughter."

"Even with the antenna, I don't think we could get a Sacramento signal here."

Colt thought it over. "He must have made it out and come this way."

Dani leaned close. "Do you really think he's right? Can we get through this?"

"If we can find enough like-minded people, then yes, I think we can." Colt turned back to Harvey. "If you really want to stop Colonel Jarvis and his men, I'll help. It won't be easy. Hell, we might be signing our death warrants. But if you all want to take a stand, I'll stand beside you."

Melody spoke up. "Why? Why help us?"

"For one, you helped me. You could have left me in the street to die, but you risked your safety to bring me here and take care of me. Two, you've kept Dani safe."

He paused, choosing his next words carefully. "But more importantly, you're all willing to fight. It's easy to surrender. It's harder than hell to fight back."

Harvey stood and closed the distance between them. He held out his hand and smiled. "Welcome to the Resistance."

ACKNOWLEDGMENTS

Thank you for reading *Chaos Comes*, book four in the *After the EMP* saga. I hoped you enjoyed reading Colt and Dani's story of finding each other and bonding despite the struggles they faced.

A huge thank you to all of my readers who are on this journey with me. Your words of encouragement humble and amaze me every day.

If you enjoyed this book and have a moment, please consider leaving a review on Amazon. Every one helps new readers discover my work and helps me keep writing the stories you want to read.

I'll be back with another installment in the *After the EMP* saga soon.

Until next time,

Harley

ALSO BY HARLEY TATE

Have you read *Darkness Falls*, the exclusive companion short story to the *After the EMP* series? If not you can get it for free by subscribing to my newsletter:

www.harleytate.com/subscribe

If you were hundreds of miles from home when the world ended, how would you protect your family?

Walter started his day like any other by boarding a commercial jet, ready to fly the first leg of his international journey. Halfway to Seattle, he witnesses the unthinkable: the total loss of power as far as he can see.

Hundreds of miles from home, he'll do whatever it takes to

get back to his wife and teenage daughter. Landing the plane is only the beginning.

ABOUT HARLEY TATE

When the world as we know it falls apart, how far will you go to survive?

Harley Tate writes edge-of-your-seat post-apocalyptic fiction exploring what happens when ordinary people are faced with impossible choices.

Harley's first series, *After the EMP*, follows the Sloane family and their friends as they try to survive in a world without power. When the nation's power grid is wrecked, it doesn't take long for society to fall apart. The end of life as we know it brings out the best and worst in all of us.

The apocalypse is only the beginning.

Contact Harley directly at:

www.harleytate.com
harley@harleytate.com

Made in the USA
San Bernardino, CA
06 November 2017